A Variety of Folk

A compilation
of short stories and poems by

Kenneth James

ISBN 978-0-9954608-0-5
Copyright ©2017 Kenneth James

A CIP record for this book is available from the British Library

This work is a work of fiction. Names and characters are the product of the
author's imagination and any resemblance to actual persons, living or dead
is entirely coincidental.

Published by
Llyfrau Cambria Books, Wales, United Kingdom.
Cambria Books is a division of
The Cambria Publishing Co-operative Ltd

Discover our other books at: www.cambriabooks.co.uk

Cover design by Carolyn Michel

Stories & Poems

Sharing

The conversation took place when Mrs Southgate had stopped Delia and Mat as they strolled through the village. They stood on the narrow pavement as the noisy traffic rushed by.

"It's true, I'm telling you. There are to be no more burials in Pant. They're thinking of opening a new cemetery near the Gurnos, or somewhere else."

The well-groomed Delia felt betrayed. "I've always lived in Pant," she said softly.

"I've been lucky," continued Mrs Southgate. "I went to the Civic Centre six months ago and bought a used plot. I'm seventy and I like to know where I'm ending up."

Delia turned to Mat, "We should be thinking about the inevitable, you know." Mat stroked his grey moustache but said nothing. Delia turned back to Mrs Southgate. "Mat and I are both sixty." Delia paused as a huge juggernaut making for the local Spar drowned her voice. "You never know when it will happen, do you? I've always thought I'd be buried in Pant."

Mat suddenly realised the situation, stepping on to the road to leave a young girl pass by. "I don't want to be buried in the Gurnos. Are you sure all the grave spaces are gone?"

Delia pulled on Mat's arm as a car raced down the road. "Get on the pavement. You'll be buried before your time," she said.

"Motorists!" snapped Mrs Southgate, staring hard at the fast driver as he sped away. "They look at you as though you shouldn't be out and about. And the fumes are enough to gas you." She tightened her headscarf. "All the new spaces are taken, Mat," she said, coming back to the subject. "But there may be an old grave with just one body. They are opening such graves for people who don't mind being buried in the same plot. Personally, I don't mind being buried with somebody as long as it's in Pant."

Delia looked at Mat. "I wouldn't mind that, would you, Mat?"

Mat puckered his lips. "I want to know who's down there. Could be a mass murderer."

Mrs Southgate shook her head dismissing the remark. "Get down to the council offices," she ordered. "They're very nice people down there; very helpful. You might be lucky." She looked up and down the road, raised her hand as a farewell gesture, then crossed when she thought it safe. "Take my advice now or you'll miss out," she called, as she was halfway across, then had to hurry as a motorbike came roaring towards her.

Mat smiled on one side of his face, "I think she's wise booking her place early," he said, a cryptic tone in his voice.

"What do you think Mat, seriously?"

"Well, I must admit, I'd feel more at home being buried locally, I suppose. And it's near the Pant-Cad-Ivor Inn," he smiled. "I could always nip out for a pint."

"Will you be sensible for just one minute? What shall we do?"

Mat looked to the grey sky and imagined the blue vastness beyond the clouds. "We'll make arrangements, my love."

The following day Delia and Mat visited the Civic Centre and made enquiries at Reception. The receptionist, an attractive dark-haired girl, kindly telephoned the relevant department who said they could give the couple an interview. The directions the receptionist gave took Mat and Delia down to the basement and into a peaceful room where three elderly ladies sat behind their individual desks. The three looked up and smiled but said nothing. The lady behind the nearest desk peered over her dark-rimmed glasses and beckoned them to sit in the two chairs opposite her; they obeyed, slowly and silently. In a very quiet voice, she said, "What can I do for you?"

Delia looked at Mat, wanting him to take the proceedings.

"Just making enquiries really," said Mat, feeling uneasy about the situation. "We were told by a friend that the council has stopped burying at Pant Cemetery. My wife and I have always lived in Pant, and though we... we're not thinking of departing just yet, but we were hoping to... sort of... stay in Pant."

"My family have always been buried in Pant," said Delia. "I'd feel a stranger if I was buried elsewhere."

The lady smiled kindly again and spoke in a sympathetic calmness, "My name is Mrs Llewellyn. We have many enquiries from people wanting to reserve a grave space. Lots of people are far younger than you. It is true however we have run out of new grave spaces. But we do have a few used graves left. If you wish to purchase a shared grave I may be able to arrange that for you."

Mat was encouraged by the lady's soft tone and accommodating manner. "Would I be indelicate if I wanted to know who was down there."

Delia looked at Mat. "Mat!"

Mrs Llewellyn gave a broad smile. "That's all right. You'd be surprised what people say when they reserve a grave space. Some want to know if there is a killer down there."

Mat shuffled awkwardly in his chair. "So it wouldn't be allowed to tell us, then?"

"I will be able to inform you of the occupant when I have located a space. I'm afraid there will be no choice, however, because there are only a few left." She paused and smiled. "You'd be surprised how funny and fussy some people are. I had one old gentleman who purchased a space and told me, "I hope my grave won't be too far from the main gates because my legs aren't very strong." I thought he was joking, but he was very serious. Anyway, I'll take your details and make a search for you. When, and if, I find some room, I will write to you. I need to have your name, address and the required fee, I'm afraid."

When the business was completed Delia and Mat thanked her for her time and kindness. As they left, the three ladies gave a final smile. Mat ensured he closed the door quietly, not wanting to disturb the tranquillity that pervaded the room.

A few days later a letter arrived from the council allocating Delia and Mat a grave space, ZXIV in Pant where a young child had been buried in the last century. Mat was amused by a receipt attached to the confirmation, it was headed Merthyr Tydfil County Borough, Leisure Department.

"We'll be there till Armageddon, I suppose, so it needs to be leisurely," he said.

He handed Delia the letter and sat on the settee where he resumed reading the newspaper.

Delia sat at his side, her slight figure still wrapped in her thick dressing gown. "I wonder who the child is," she thought aloud.

Mat lowered his paper, "What child?"

"The child who's buried there."

"They won't tell you that," he said, rustling his broadsheet as he lifted it again.

"It's a nice thought knowing you are going to keep a child company. I wonder if it's a boy or a girl."

"Does it make any difference what sex it is? The poor thing is just a bundle of bones now."

"The spirit is still there, waiting for company."

Mat lowered his paper again. "Waiting for the resurrection, I suppose."

"We're both Christians, Mat. That's what we are taught to believe in."

"You wouldn't like to make me a cup of tea, would you, love?"

Delia got the message as she made her way absent-minded move towards the kitchen, still thinking. "It could be. It could very well be, you know…Last century. It could be seventy or eighty years the little darling died."

Mat ruffled his paper. "What now? What could be?"

"It doesn't matter. Do you want a biscuit with your tea?"

"That will be fine."

"After you've had your tea and read your paper we'll take a trip up the cemetery and try and find this grave. I'd like to know where it is."

Mat put his paper down, deciding to get into the spirit of things. "I hope it has a pleasant view," he called. "I wouldn't want you complaining."

His facetious remark made her smile. She took off her glasses and cleaned them after the kettle had steamed them. Carrying a cup of tea to Mat, she placed it on the coffee table at his side.

"I'm going to get ready for the cemetery," she said. She turned and smiled at him. "I hope the neighbours are nice."

Mat chuckled and sipped his tea. "There'll be no barbecues or noisy music, anyway."

As it was a fine autumn day but chilly, they dressed in warm clothes and walked to the cemetery. They called into the office behind the cemetery church and asked the supervisor for directions.

"It's a little complicated," he said, taking his glasses off and standing up. "But I've got to go and see if the boys are digging, so I'll take you."

He was a short man of slight build but walked sprightly. They strode in single file on a steep narrow rising path, parallel to a stone wall overlooking the main road. The tarmac gradient became steeper and the increasing pace of the man soon made Delia and Mat gasp heavily. Mat peered over the wall and realised the ten-foot drop was too close for comfort. Being safety conscious he used the top of the wall as hand rail with his left hand and towed Delia behind him with his right hand. On the right was an array of pitted headstones, grey and lichened. There was not one gravestone which stood erect and straight. Arched pieces of granite tilted to all points of the compass. Huge stone crosses leaned forward looking tired and worn, oblong tombs subsided sadly. At the top, the path wound around and came to narrow crossroad. There, the supervisor stopped and pointed to a piece of rough grass between two crumbling headstones. There was no sign of identification, and the long lumpy couch grass was turning autumn yellow.

"It doesn't look much, I'm afraid. It's been abandoned for a long time. I'll leave you to it and check on my diggers over the other side."

"Thank you," puffed Delia.

"It's a pleasure," he said, and went on his way.

Mat looked around him regaining his composure and taking in the scenery. They were at the top all right, gravestones all around, sloping down on all sides. Scattered here and there, standing proudly among the old crosses and tombs, like new boys on the block, were shining black granite headstones indicating the recently interred. There was a fine view of the bleak Twynau Mountains and the wind-swept ridges. Down the slope he could see a piece of ground covered with fresh wreaths and sprays. Delia just stood gazing at the unkempt piece of six by three.

"Mat, can you feel an atmosphere?"

Mat pulled at his flat cap. "What atmosphere?"

"Well, you know, as though there's something about the plot that's drawn us here."

"£130, that's what's drawn me here. We've had our money's worth. There's a fine view and the neighbours are quiet"

"Fate. I feel as though fate has drawn us to this spot for some reason."

Mat turned his back on her, not to ignore her, but to shelter his behind from the strong chilly breeze. Coming through the gates on the Bryniau side was a hearse accompanied by the funeral cortege.

"Here we come. In a few years they'll be bringing us in like that."

"Us?" questioned Delia. "We're going to die the same day, are we?"

"I didn't think of that. If you want the top bunk you'd better hope I go first. They won't remake the bed once you're in."

"Try and take things seriously, Mat."

"You've got to think of these things."

"I'm going to buy some flowers for this grave," said Delia.

Mat turned to her. "There's nothing wrong with you, is there?"

"We'll have to tidy it up. Make it look respectable."

"It's a grave, not the front lawn."

"Somebody is down there, Mat; alone and neglected. The little darling deserves respect."

"Mrs Southgate will think you're mad."

"I don't care. I have a feeling about this grave. A very deep feeling indeed."

Mat wasn't one to argue. He turned his attention back to the funeral. The open grave was surrounded with mourners looking to the sky, their lament riding strongly on the breeze.

"Let's go," he said. "I don't want to see them shovelling the earth in."

As the weeks went by the roughness of the grave was transformed into a neat and tidy rectangle: All grass had been removed and a concrete kerb surrounded the fresh brown soil. Three urns of flowers, equally spaced, made it stand out brilliantly. The diggers appeared puzzled, for they hadn't opened it up. But then their boss explained about the responsible people who had purchased it.

Mat had given up on Delia; she had become obsessed with the grave and was attempting to trace the history of it. Then one day he realised she was more relaxed about the subject, though she still went up the cemetery once a month to tidy it. He wanted to know why her enthusiasm had subsided, but didn't like to mention it in case it might re-kindle the fire. Nevertheless, one Sunday having a quiet lunch at home, he decided it was time to be logical about it again.

"Is it this Sunday for the cemetery, love?"

"Next week. I'll get some flowers on Friday."

"You've given up the atmospheric peculiarities of the grave then?"

"I know who's buried there now, don't I?"

Mat was shocked. This was the first he heard of it. "Who's buried there? Who is it?"

"I told you some force had drawn us there. Well, you didn't share my intuition. But if you remember, years ago, I told you about a young child who died in our family sometime in the last century. My grandfather told me it was his younger sister. She was only four when she passed away. It's her."

Mat was staring at her in disbelief. "How do you know it's her?"

"I researched my family. My grandfather's sister was buried in Pant cemetery, and the grave we bought was first opened the year of her death, down to the month. So it must be."

"There must have been lots of graves opened the same time."

"I dare say. But I had a dream two weeks ago. I saw the cemetery the way it would have been over a hundred years ago. I saw a child's coffin being lowered into our space. And then, I had a clear picture of my grandfather."

Mat looked up at the ceiling and then stared her straight in the eye. "You're serious, aren't you?"

"My grandparents were never ones for spending money on graves." She finished chewing on a piece of chicken and pointed her fork at him. "My relative is buried there. I know it! I know it!"

"Who am I to doubt you, love," he said, then carried on with his Sunday lunch.

"And do you know the irony of it? They have now stopped selling used graves. Fate waited for us to purchase our grave."

Mat suddenly felt a chill. It was the phrase, "Our grave." It all seemed too close for comfort.

Beached Fish

Skip sniffed the brown fish
drying on the lonely beach,
distant heaven lapped.

Rejected by a cruel wave
it lay impotent in an alien world
of humans,
Paradise lost.

I touched it with my walking stick,
its tail curled in limp communication.
A tired eye rested on me
unfolding imagery in my mind:
to carry a lost snail across a merciless
road in seconds,
to rescue a dust-crusted worm
and return it to moist soil,
or guide a panicking bee
out of a glasshouse into ethereal splendour,
had always been within my power.

I dropped the fish into the becalmed sea,
its spirit quivered to life,
then circled before it held straight,
saluting me with knowing looks.
Lingering, it faced us, its gills pulsing,
its stare transfixed, a message in its eyes:

Three of God`s creations.
If I can do for these creatures, who are
unconscious of my strength,
such easy acts of greatness,
how simple it is for the Creator
to redeem me in deathly moments
and fly me through the universe to Home.
With those thoughts warming my soul,
the fish turned and swam away.

Forgotten Danger

It's nothing to joke about, Richard.

"He's had the car just three days and already Earth people are complaining. "He's blown eighteen years of savings on a souped-up convertible sports car. Souped-up!"

"We promised he could use the money as he wanted when he came of age," said Pauline, busying herself making the last of the sandwiches.

Richard filled the kettle. "I'm going to make a cup of tea. We both saved hard for him. I thought he'd make it to university."

Pauline wrapped cling film over the last tray of sandwiches, rested her hands on the worktop and looked through the kitchen window at the autumnal garden. "Yes, he has the qualifications. Still, He's made his choice."

"You're going over the top with all this catering; decorating the hall, all these trays of food."

"We mustn't let him down on his eighteenth."

"He's changed," said Richard, brushing his hand through his shock of grey hair. "When he sits behind the wheel he goes into a trance."

Pauline began gathering bags of plastic cutlery. "All youngsters are a bit wild in their teens."

"Wild? I suspect you had an affair with a Martian before he was born."

She smiled. "It's too serious to joke about, Richard."

"He`s had the car three days and already Earth people are complaining. He rockets through the village like a demented android"

"He's our son."

"Is he? He was six years ago when he had a normal head of hair and talked to us with respect. Now He's like an extra-terrestrial Samson."

They both stiffened as they heard the sound of a speeding car coming closer with a thunderous roar. Its brakes screeched up the driveway, then a final contemptuous revving before it died.

"Be tactful, Richard, please. It's the party tonight. I Don't want bad feelings."

He came in dressed in a black arm-less T-shirt, his angular face flushed with excitement, his brown hair blown high and spiky, making him look taller than his six feet. He stood in the kitchen with his goggles misted up trying to focus.

"What is it?" said his father. "Do want to meet my leader?"

Gerwyn raised his goggles and gave a huge grin. "Nice one, Dad. Your wit is improving. Actually, I was enjoying the savoury aroma."

"Goggles Gerwyn?"

"I had the hood folded back. If you get dust in your eyes doing a ton, it could be all over in seconds."

His mother stared hard at him. "I hope you're not serious."

Richard adjusted his trousers, his bulbous stomach overlapping his belt. "Having your £5,000.00s worth, Gerwyn!."

"Not five thousand, Dad. Four thousand eight hundred and fifty I knocked him down a hundred and fifty."

His father closed his eyes, "£150.00 saved, well, well. Off shore investments I suggest."

His mother was concerned. "Gerwyn, will you drive more carefully please? she said, wiping her hands in her apron.

"Like Dad drives his Fiesta, you mean? I've been to Abergavenny and back before Dad goes for his paper and back."

"Be serious Gerwyn. You're worrying us to death."

He went and hugged his mother, her plump body compressing against her son's sturdy frame. "Don't worry, Mam. I know how to handle a car."

His father shook his head. "Remember what I taught you, son, however good a driver you are there is always an idiot around the next corner."

Gerwyn grinned. "I know, Dad. That's me."

His father gave up and left the room, forgetting about his tea. Gerwyn went to his bedroom, changed his clothes, cleaned up and then returned to the kitchen. He pinched a half pasty from a plateful, eliciting a gentle tap on the wrist from his mother. She looked at him. His hair combed, his handsome face shining, and a new sky-blue sweat shirt clinging to him.

"Gerwyn, I'm proud of the way you've grown into a clean and strong young man, but you must realise there's a lot to learn in life."

He ignored the maternal cliché. "Nice taste on this pasty. Is the club function room sorted for tonight, Mam?"

"It's all arranged."

"Pity you couldn't get it for Saturday, Dad could have slept late."

"Sunday was the only date available."

"I suggested he take the next day off but he won't."

"He's proud of his attendance record."

Gerwyn looked at the trays full of pasties, sandwiches, sausage rolls, trifles, vol-au-vents and admired the six gateaus, three Strawberry and three Black forests.

"You've worked hard, Mam." I appreciate it. How are you going to get the food down to the club?"

"Your father and your uncle Fred are taking two car loads down, then bringing the cars home. But you can help."

"Of course I will. I've got loads of friends coming. It's going to be a great night."

"Your auntie Mary's been helping, along with cousin Rhian."

Gerwyn noted a different tone in her voice. "That sounds more like an overture than a statement."

"I'm worried, Gerwyn. Auntie Mary informs me you frightened a young child when you drove through the village yesterday."

"Stupid boy was playing chicken."

"You were going very fast."

"That's what sports cars are made for. If I wanted to meander around the roads I'd buy a scooter."

His mother caught him by the shoulders and turned him to face her. "What if you had hit the child? Or worse, killed him!"

"No way! I was in complete command of the situation."

"Where have I heard that, before? Gerwyn, I'm begging you, please drive slower."

Gerwyn gave her a peck on the cheek. "I'll be more careful."

"Promise me, son."

"I promise. Now stop fussing."

* * *

The spacious hall was full, a mixture of age groups, but mostly

12

youngsters in their late teens. The congratulations, handshakes and pats on the back had all been done. So had the cutting of the birthday cake and the singing of the birthday song. The buffet had been consumed completely which left Pauline wondering had she under catered, but Gerwyn assured her everything was going wonderfully. The disco music was thumping out the bass tones, vibrating through the hall, and the floor was packed with robotic people making all kinds of movements with their limbs. Richard had been drinking with his contemporaries hoping nobody would come up with a new complaint about his son`s driving, but it was playing on his mind more than anyone else. However, as the alcohol took over and pictures of his son bombing around the roads kept going through his mind, he thought he'd have a quiet word. Gerwyn was on the side-lines talking to a girl when Richard approached him, rather unsteadily.

"Are you going to acquaint me, son"?"

"You've had a few, Dad."

"Always enjoy a party. Well, acquaint me."

"Well, my name's Gerwyn, and this is my eighteenth birthday party."

His father groaned. The blonde girl at Gerwyn's side dug her elbow into him and smiled.

"Sorry Dad," said Gerwyn, adopting a serious manner. "This is an old school friend, Dawn."

"I was hoping your name was Delilah."

Dawn appeared confused. "Oh. His hair, you mean."

Gerwyn grinned. "Ignore him. This is my Dad. He worries a lot."

"With you as a son, that's hardly surprising. Nice to meet you Mr Monroe," said Dawn. "I was about to mingle so I'll leave you and Gerwyn to have a father and son chat."

"Nice to meet you Dawn, if you get a chance, buy a pair of scissors...." She gave a cute twiddle of her fingers, then left.

"Gerwyn, let's go into the bar away from this noise and have a drink with me," invited Richard."

Gerwyn felt uneasy. "Now Dad, you're not going to spoil the night."

"No, no, now listen, I know I promised not to raise the subject, but," he paused. "Why Don't you sell your car and get a more conventional one?"

Gerwyn laughed loudly and put his arm around his father.

"Come on, Dad. Buy me a pint. We'll make a deal, I won't nag you to take a day off tomorrow if you won't mention my car. Tomorrow you go to work and I'll go for a drive around the country roads."

"I'll make a better deal. I won't go to work tomorrow if you have a day off from driving your car."

"No way! Come on, where's that drink?"

They went to the bar and bought a round each, both drinking without mentioning the car. It was Gerwyn who spoke first.

"I love your company, Dad, but, you're no competition for Dawn."

His father nodded. "Off you go."

"Did you manage to get an extension for tonight?"

"Twelve midnight, officially."

* * *

Pauline was pale-faced and anxious as she sat in the waiting room of the emergency operating theatre. She was unaware of the hubbub of the busy department. Outside the room trolleys were being pushed hurriedly, doctors and nurses were calling to each other, telephones were ringing. But she was trying to hold back the tears by quietly mumbling to herself. "What's going to happen...Lord Don't let him die.....I can't....I can't believe it.....last night he was so happy...."

Just then a doctor, still gowned up, came in and sat at her side. "I'm sorry it's been a long wait for you Mrs Monroe, but he sustained many injuries and needed some work."

"How is he, doctor? Is he all right?"

"He's been transferred to the Intensive Therapy Unit but I'm confident he will fine. The bad news is he has broken both an arm and a leg. He also has broken ribs and there's multiple bruising, plus some stitching around his head. He was lucky to escape with his life."

"Intensive Therapy Unit doctor?"

"Just precautionary. He hasn't come round from the anaesthetic. Once they've stabilised him he'll go to a ward. I Don't wish to add to your trauma, but it's best you hear from me than other sources."

Pauline appeared puzzled. "Hear what, doctor?"

"Road accidents have to be reported to the police. The fact is, there was a high level of alcohol in his blood; far over the legal limit. I'd rather

14

tell you before the police break the news."

Pauline dropped her head. "If only I didn't have the party."

The doctor touched her hand. "Anyway, I'm sure they'll let you into ITU for a few minutes. Where is the young man who came with you?"

"He's had to go and sign for some personal things down at Casualty."

"Shall I get a nurse to sit with you?"

Pauline didn't hear the question. "They had their differences, you know. My husband and son, I mean...but they love each other."

"I'm sure they do. Is there anything I can do for you?"

"Poor Gerwyn, he was so happy yesterday. On top of the world he was, and now, well..." She buried her head in her hands. "He blames himself."

Just then Gerwyn came in, his face ashen, his eyes glassy. As he sat at his mother's side and placed his arm around her, the doctor left.

"I feel responsible, Mam."

His mother hugged him. "Don't ever think that."

"He wanted to make a deal with me. He said he'd have a day off from work if I had a day off driving my car. If only I'd agreed."

His mother crushed him to her and rocked him. "I told him not to go to work. He was wreaking of whisky as he left the house."

Gerwyn broke away and looked at her. "The police were down Accident & Emergency. They had a chat with me. They said no other vehicle was involved."

Why did he go the country road way?" asked his mother.

"He knew, Mam. He must have felt groggy going to work. We shouldn't have continued the party at home. The police said he wasn't fit to be in charge of a vehicle. He hit a corner of a stone wall. He didn't even have his seat belt on."

"Thirty years he's been driving and not a scratch."

"He was probably wondering about me and the car."

"Come on, son. Let's go and see him."

"Every birthday will be an anniversary of his accident," said Gerwyn. "It will be like a sick birthday card coming through the door."

Old Railroad

On a foggy day my dog and I
climbed soggy banks to the old railway line.
Forsaken, peaceful, in disrepair,
no high-pitched whistle to scare
you scrambling as in youthful days.
The silence was broken by a lonely sparrow
purring from bush to bush.
The sleeperless, railless, gravelled gully,
sheltered by precipitous couch-grass banks,
sparkled with an eerie encampment
made brighter by the heavy September mist:
Spread around and up the slopes,
like tops of four-poster beds,
glittered cobwebs laden with dew.
Scattered sheets glistened with tiny crystal balls,
silky hammocks hung in bramble bushes
from the glow of the rose hip
to the lanterns on the gorse.
Threads of gossamer guy lines, shining with droplets,
stretched from the purple-flowering thistle
to the globe of the dandelion,
from meadow sweet to whinberry,
ragwort to heather,
all pegged down to the clover.
The spectral weather had lit the nomad's lights.
Not a spider in sight nor a movement perceived,
but the sense of a tribe surviving the
stillness of the aftermath.
What was left of life was hiding.

The Faulty Cooker

Trevor made his rounds collecting his job-slips. At the depot, his foreman insisted his jobs had priority. In the showroom the assistant gave him a coy smile and cooed, "please do my jobs first, darling." He gave her a hopeful wink. Upstairs in the multi-desk office where perfume and cigarette smoke fused and telephones trilled, the ageing blonde ruffled his hair and called him a handsome rascal. "Do those jobs first and I'll give you a big kiss." As always, he arranged his jobs in geographical order.

Passing the Engineer's office, Jack called him from the open door. Trevor stopped and leaned on the door jamb.

"I'm a busy man Jack, got lots to get through."

"Stop bulling! Come in, and sit down," he drawled.

Jack leaned back in his swivel chair looking at the ceiling, twiddling his biro. Trevor felt inferior sitting there in his duffel coat and brown overalls. Jack was meticulous; Smart navy suit, white shirt and a small knot in his blue tie.

Trevor lost patience. "I've got ten jobs to get through and that's the truth. They're all marked urgent."

"I've come through the ranks. Been on the tools, and in the night-schools," he rhymed, smiling on one side of his face as he dropped his gaze to Trevor. "I've got a job that's urgent—how old are you Trev?"

"Twenty two."

"I'm forty two. I've done everything you've done but a thousand times over." His hands fell on the arms of his swivel chair and he made half turns. "A nut-case reckons he's going to throw his cooker through the showroom window. How's that for urgency?"

Trevor scratched his forehead. "I don't like the sound of this."

With a challenging stare, Jack leaned forward, the sweetness of his Brylcream wafting across to Trevor. "All in an electrician's day, Trev." He sat back. "I've been to the customer's home and carried out tests. I'm afraid I couldn't impress the guy."

"I don't see what I…"

"If we gave a new cooker to everyone who complained just because

17

it's under guarantee... Well, we'd all be out of a job, including service sparks."

"So what can I do?"

"This Jones guy claims his cooker's not as good as it was when new. He also takes a dim view of white collar officials. A boiler-suited worker doing a few technical checks might be more on his level."

Trevor stared hard. "How come this is the first I've heard of the job."

"He came ranting into the showrooms a couple of days ago demanding to see the top dog. I told him I'd personally see to it. Later, I paid him a visit, checked his cooker and told him there was nothing wrong with it. He showed me to the door."

Trevor grimaced. "You expect me to sort it out?"

"I've been keeping an eye on you, Trev. You have a way with customers. I know you'll do your best for the Company."

Trevor knew if he refused he would be in bad books for a long time. "I'll give it a go, but any aggression and I'll be off."

The bitter February weather was blustery with powdery snow stinging his eyes. The roads were treacherous, the traffic busy. He arrived at the council estate hoping for a "no-answer." He got in his van and drove off. He drove through the monotonous estate: all houses cream, some with graffiti, all doors maroon. He found the house, grabbed his tool bag and stepped out into a slushy gutter.

A six-foot burly chap opened the door wearing only a white vest and baggy trousers. Trevor guessed he was mid-fifties. His bald head rested on his short thick neck pushing between broad shoulders. He stared at Trevor with bulbous eyes, waiting.

"I'm from the Cooker Company, Mr Jones."

He had a deep snarling voice. "I'm not illiterate, son, your van makes it quite clear where you're from. So they've sent me a scrawny kid."

"Sorry, but my boss, the man who came up, asked me to have a look at your cooker."

"He's a boss? God help you if he's the brains of the outfit."

Trevor shrugged his shoulders.

"He's been pushing pens too long. Listen, Mr Jones, if I can't find the fault, I'll recommend a new cooker."

Jones squinted at him. "Your boss said my wife should be pleased with the new cooker." He spat on the path. "My wife's been dead for two years."

Trevor suddenly felt uncomfortable. "I'm sorry to hear that. I'm completely neutral, Mr Jones. I sympathise with you but I'm just a worker."

"I know that, boy. I'm not stupid." He didn't move from the doorway.

"If you dump the cooker in the showroom that's fine with me, but I've got to check it over."

"Listen son, I didn't like that clever dick coming up here trying to pull the wool over my eyes."

Trevor detected a slight mellowing. Plaintively he asked, "Can I come in and do a few tests, please?"

Jones huffed, spat on the path again and went inside, mumbling, "No point in taking it out on you."

The kitchen was as clinical as a hospital. A strong pungent smell of bleach pervaded the room. It seemed to be everywhere. The cooker had been washed down with it, so had the draining board, worktops, and the floor, he suspected. Jones was clearly honouring his wife's memory. Trevor switched on the four radiant rings, the oven and the grill. They all worked perfectly. He tested the temperature of the oven, the cut-out times of the thermostat, checked the internal wiring and mains supply. Jones leaned on the door frame throughout. He seemed more interested in Trevor than the cooker.

"I've seen you before!" he said

Trevor looked up. "You look familiar." But he was unsure.

"Have you always worked for this Company?"

"I served my time in a factory."

He smiled remembering. "You used to come in the Auto shop with the Sparks, carrying his toolbox."

Trevor sneezed, the bleach was getting stronger. "You worked on those machines? I tried to avoid that place. It was deafening and greasy, with a blue oily mist in the air."

"That's the place. I ran the big automatic. I was the setter/operator. Nobody could look after that machine like me."

"We didn't have much trouble with it, fair play."

"You had a nice little number there, boy?"

Trevor shook his head. "I'm practically my own boss driving around. Are you still working there?"

Jones seemed thoughtful. "I had to finish to look after my wife—What's the verdict on the cooker?"

Trevor sighed. "I can't find anything wrong."

"Surprise, surprise," but there was a light-hearted tone in his voice.

Trevor didn't like failing. "I tell you what, put the kettle on the ring. Let's go through the actions."

He squinted in a friendly way. "I'm not bloody stupid."

"I could murder a cup of tea?"

"I'll make you a cup of tea, son, if the tap's not frozen. I waited two hours yesterday for the council plumber to thaw out the damn thing." The tap worked. He filled the kettle and placed it on the cooker. "That kettle will take twice as long to boil than it did when I first bought the cooker."

Trevor thought for a while and then grinned as the penny dropped. "Is that it, Mr Jones? Is that your complaint?"

"The longer it takes to boil, the more it costs me in electricity, innit?

"When did you buy the cooker?"

"It's under guarantee. It's only seven months old."

Trevor thought again, calculating. "Which means you bought it July-August time?"

"What's that got to do with it?"

Would he offend him, Trevor wondered. He'd have to tread carefully, but he's got to know the truth. "In Summer, Mr Jones," he began tentatively, "the water is tepid coming through the tap. In February, it comes out like liquid ice. It's bound to take longer to boil."

Jones went silent, his face reddening. It was only the past month he had noticed the problem. He felt foolish. He took the lid off the kettle and stuck his finger in. "Why didn't that dick-of-a- boss think of that? "

Trevor wondered why Jones hadn't thought of it. "Summer will bring your cooker back to its true potential, Mr Jones, I guarantee it."

"Ice-cold water! Well, well, well. Oh hell!" He was distant again, thinking, his eyes sparkling fire. "I'll pay that fool of a boss of yours a visit tomorrow; He should know the difference between summer and winter water!"

Trevor didn't want that. "Leave it to me," he said, "I shall mention it at the right moment in front of the right people. Guarantee complete embarrassment"

Jones smiled, he liked the idea. "Okay, fair enough—are you going to wait for the kettle and have a cuppa?"

"Why not, it's cold out there."

"I'll treat you to one of my home-made Welshcakes."

Trevor blinked his stinging eyes. Welshcakes flavoured with bleach.

The Velvet Path

For those times when we feel less than we are,
ill-humoured by life`s crude events,
we must hold in reserve a great happiness,
keeping fresh the joy of our summer scents.
Not those stale occasions
when we sit in mediocre comfort,
indulging in simple glories,
abiding in tepid pretence.
I mean those ecstatic moments of bliss;
wanting no more than we have.
When souls surmount all worldly fears and
no power in the universe can put us down:

The spiritual consummation of youthful days
when bodies and hearts are fused together,
after being suspended in second-hand dreams.
She had been created for me and was
out there somewhere waiting to be found;
frustrated by demands for education,
confused by standards of civilisation.
To throw away precious time on such
adult trivialities was irrelevant.
She, who was created to make me whole,
was there amid a million faces,
having her head turned away
by teachers and preachers.

One ordinary day, with youthful company,
in the meadow of the velvet path,
when nothing was special in the cosmos,
I kissed a girl light-heartedly.
In that moment of impetuous fun
Nature`s pass-word entered our hearts.
Closed eyes spoke through sealed lips,
telepathy bonded our bodies with love.
It was the lifting from the cold abyss
to the warmest peak of perfection.
Now, in winter, with perfumed flames,
We warm ourselves with teenage days.

Adventure Playground

Donald said. "Nobody will bother us up the tips."

"It's too wet and muddy up there," Tommy reminded him."

"The last thing my mother said was, don't go up the tips" said Jimmy, "so I'm not going up there. We need to find somewhere nice and dry."

"The Lukie is our best bet," suggested Tommy. "If we're quiet, Lukie Lou might let us sit there."

"Lou does the nights," said Jimmy. "Gasping Glyn does the afternoon."

"The tips are a better bet," insisted Donald. "Nobody'll bother us up there. My mother doesn't like me going to the Lukie."

"And my mother doesn't like me going up the tips," argued Jimmy. "Come on, Let's get in the dry."

The three nine-year-olds crept up to the first floor of the Lucania and crouched on the landing outside the snooker room, ensuring they remained below the window of the half glazed door. They sat for some time until their curiosity got the better of them, then they held the door ajar and peered in. Lights above the eight tables dropped smoky shrouds on the thin green baize; dirty yellow patches highlighted the vacant nap. However, the open door attracted the attention of the manager who moved forward to investigate.

"Look out! He's coming," warned Donald.

Donald and Tommy ran down the stairs thudding and slipping on the wooden steps. Jimmy held his ground, now standing cheekily, watching the games through the glass panel of the door, listening to the balls clicking and the language of the players. The ageing manager pulled the door fully open, a cigarette stuck to his pale wet lips.

"You're a brazen little brat, aren't you," he said, his lungs bubbling as he fought for breath.

The smoky staleness of the room flowed out as Jimmy studied the lined face of the man. He thought he detected softness behind the haziness of his tired eyes.

"I'm not doing any harm and it's wet outside. Can I come in? I'll sit quietly, honest."

The man was sharp and positive. "No you can't! Go and play in the park," he rasped, then took the cigarette from his mouth and gave a rattling cough. Jimmy turned and thudded slowly and deliberately down the stairs.

Outside, Donald and Tommy waited in the doorway of Turner's shoe shop until Jimmy came. The three, hands in pockets, sheltered in the deep recess of the entrance. Earlier, the August weather had been overcast but dry and warm. Now their short trousers, shirts and sleeveless jumpers were proving to be inadequate for the drizzling afternoon. Looking miserable and dejected, they observed the hustle and bustle of Upper Union Street.

A man carried empty wooden trays on his head to his van outside Ferrari's cafe. Women hurried on their way, arms hanging with heavy bags, others in couples chatted. Four men hung out on the corner near the chemist. Two puffed on cigarettes, two had their hands behind their backs, oblique and glum.

"This is really boring," complained Donald. My mother doesn't like me hanging around the streets. If we're not going up the park, Let's go up the tips."

"The park is even more boring," said Tommy, struggling to wipe his nose on his shoulder. "It's for little kids."

Jimmy began inspecting the brown and black shoes hanging on a long string outside the door but sheltered in the recess. He shadow-boxed them, but hit them too hard making them swing and clunk the window.

"Oye! Clear off you lot," called a man from the inside.

They ran off up Union Street and turned right down Wind Street then jumped through the puddle-ridden car park behind the Oddfellows Hall. They crossed old gardens of empty condemned houses where rocks broke through the earth like bald heads. An abandoned tabby sat on a half collapsed wall crouching in a defensive position and hissing as they passed.

They came out by the Bush Hotel, crossed the main road, infuriating drivers, and sat on the rails in the bus terminus at the top of The Goat Mill Road; a road that led to the factories. A double decker pulled out on its way to Merthyr. Jimmy raced after it, jumped on the platform and swung around the vertical bar. The conductor came charging up the aisle clutching his leather money pouch and ticket machine, but Jimmy jumped off as the bus picked up speed.

"Come on," urged Donald, running down the Goat Mill Road, "Let's make for the tips.

"I'm not going up the tips," insisted Jimmy. "My mother put me straight into the bath last Saturday."

"The old works will be more interesting," Tommy said.

"Yea, We'll sail on the pond," agreed Jimmy.

"It`ll be drier in the old railway wagon up the tips," said Donald. " Maybe the big boys are playing cards."

"We`re going to the old works," emphasised Tommy. "So Don't keep on about the tips."

They climbed steep iron steps to forbidden areas, wound their way up a narrow gully flanked by high slag banks, crept past the rear of the Candlewick factory and finally rested near the front of the great red-brick engine house. They lay on their stomachs behind a grassless mound thirty yards from the large open doors of the high-built workshop. By now their faces were smudged, their hands black, their clothes wet and dirty. Distant clanging and bright flashes exploded inside the engine house, sparks lit up the multi-window front. Workmen turned their unprotected eyes to the doorways.

"Wait until they look back inside," said Tommy "Then run like mad."

They got away across the huge forecourt as shouts of warning echoed from the workmen. The boys continued into the maze of the old Dowlais Works wasteland. They ran over mounds of rubble, climbed rusting railway wagons, axles still pungent with thick grease, jumped over rivulets of black water streaked with toxic greens and oranges. Remains of collapsed yellow-brick walls revealed where factory workshops once stood. Further on they stopped and looked down into a large murky hollow. The area was silent except for the panting of the boys.

"That's the biggest pond around here," gasped Tommy, pointing into the depression at an oil-skimmed pool, thirty feet in diameter. "There's a couple of old railway sleepers over there. We'll tie them together and float across. There should be rope around here somewhere, the big boys used it last Saturday."

It began to drizzle again. The sleepers, rotten and flaked, were manageable. While Jimmy and Tommy worked on the raft, Donald was told to keep a look-out. He got bored and shot-putted rocks into the pond splotching the grey slime, concentric circles slurped to the edge.

With the raft completed and ready for christening, Jimmy volunteered to give it a test run. When he was half way across the pool Tommy looked up and saw a large figure on a mound of gravel in the distance making towards them. "Watchman, watchman!" he yelled, then he and Donald took off. Jimmy tried to jump to the bank but missed by a couple of feet. Splashed with filthy water he ran after his mates. He managed to get out of the hollow and down to a gully, but he could hear the watchman's heavy boots thudding behind him. Confused, he ran between two yellow-brick walls six feet apart and just as high. There was no way out, he had to go forward. He glanced behind and realised the watchman was getting closer. A picture stuck in his mind: Black beard, burning eyes, big man breathing hatred. He told his legs to go faster, but they became weaker. Then his body began to tingle with pins and needles, his shoulders ached, his arms fell heavily to his sides. Before him was a six-foot wall across the gully blocking his exit making him panic into a cold sweat. He must run faster and jump high to grip the top of the wall, but by the time he reached there he could only crash into it and fall to the ground. He turned around on his knees, breathless and defeated, waiting to be dragged to his feet and beaten.

The watchman towered over Jimmy and stared at the gasping pale-faced kid, the thin features lined with exhaustion, the blue eyes fearful yet defiant. The man bent down, caught Jimmy by his coat lapels and hauled him to his feet. Jimmy could see the saliva congealed around the corner of the man's lips breaking through the black bristles of his beard as he sucked in volumes of breath.

"I'm not going to hurt you, son, but you shouldn't be here, he gasped. "This place is a death trap." He turned Jimmy around, caught him by the seat of his pants and collar of his jumper, then gently lifted him to the top of the wall. Jimmy scrambled over as the man's voice thundered after him, "If I catch you over here again I'll give you a damn good hiding."

He walked slowly to a tump of grass and sat, breathing heavily, his body weak, his arms and legs tingling, his thoughts on his mates who had deserted him. There he sat, confused and alone, until his strength returned

Wet and exhausted, he crossed a flat stretch of gravelled land avoiding the engine house. Ahead he could see his two mates waving from the top of a steep coal tip. He climbed the tip and wearily sat down drawing in oxygen. "You're sneaks. You're a couple of sneaks," he managed to splutter.

Tommy felt guilty. "If we had waited he would have caught the three of us. Did he belt you?"

"Yea. He give me a damn good hiding. I managed to kick him in the shins and escape."

"We won't go there again," said Donald. "Let's go up the tips. Maybe the big boys are playing cards."

"They won't let you play unless You've got two bob," said Tommy.

"I know where their hideout is. It's near the big Blackie. If you make a noise they'll let you play just to shut you up."

"I feel weak," said Jimmy.

"You'll feel better in the wagon up the tips," insisted Donald. "Come on, we're half way there."

"I suppose we could go for a half hour," agreed Jimmy, too washed out to argue.

And so, Donald had his way and they scrambled over the coal tips until they found the old railway wagon. However, by the time they got there, the big boys were on their way home, having had their illegal card game and ready for food. After a brief rest in the old railway wagon they decided to go home.

The trio reached Jimmy's street realising they needed an alibi for the disgusting state they were in and agreed they had been playing in the park all afternoon. Jimmy invited his mates in to verify the alibi. As they entered the house Jimmy's mother screamed, "Stop! Don't come any further. Take your shoes off." They did and went in.

His mother stood there akimbo with thunder on her face. "You've been up those coal tips!"

"No we haven't Mam, honest, said Jimmy. "You said you needed space to do the housework so we went up the park."

"Down the sewer more like it."

"Up the park, Mrs Morgan," said Tommy, the more convincing liar of the three. "The rain has made it all muddy. And the big boys were pushing and shoving us"

"And somebody put grease on the slide," said Donald, quietly, lacking conviction. "I think we should have gone up the tips. My mother doesn't like me going to the Lukie."

"You've been up the Lukie?"

"No, Mam," said Jimmy sadly. "We wandered around Union Street for a while, then up the park. I tried to stay out as long as possible for you, Mam. But I began to feel cold and wet."

Mrs Morgan looked at the three rain-soaked youngsters and felt a pang of guilt. "I didn't expect you to play in the rain, Jimmy. It was dry when you went out. You should have come home."

The three boys looked forlorn and gazed pitifully at her.

"Can I stay in, Mam?"

"Of course, my little love. You're good boys, really, aren't you? Take off those wet clothes and I'll make a nice cup of hot cocoa for the three of you."

The Seed

It falls unnoticed to the ground;

a powerful speck of biology.

Naked, helpless, kicked and trodden,

frost will bite and snow will fall.

But come the spring it conquers all

and blossoms into glory.

Trusting

With his desk facing the door and the computer on a shelf behind him, he felt secure sitting in the swivel chair between the two. If someone should enter the office he'd cover his mouth with a sheet of paper and peer over it with brown suspicious eyes, such was the depth of Fred's embarrassment caused by halitosis. His blue striped tie did nothing for his shirt, a thick tan garment which frequently had one collar turned up. When told the Administrator wanted to see him, he'd throw his pager into the drawer and announce, "I'm going to inspect my troops."

Fred turned to his computer and perused the list of names and shift patterns displayed there; cost-cutting was top of the agenda. Then the office door flew open, but he ignored the intrusion. Only one man has the audacity to burst in, Arnold Northover, his Junior Engineer. Northover placed a new aerosol can on the desk.

"£1.99." he said, then began looking through some books on a nearby shelf .

"What do you want with my books?" demanded Fred, who was very sensitive of anyone handling his property.

"I need the Health & Safety Regulations."

Fred swung around, a suspicious frown on his angular face. To him the Health & Safety Regulations always had hidden meanings between the lines and were treacherous. He pulled a crumpled handkerchief from his pocket, held it to his mouth and stared at his six-foot junior engineer. Northover irritated him. He loped about the hospital smartly dressed with an important air, his red-cheeked, cherubic face was not consistent with the macho image of his electrical "troops".

"What's happened? Tell me!" his voice muffled by the handkerchief.

"Nothing's happened, Fred. I need to switch off the power down the doctors residential for final connection to the new street lighting."

"Black out the residential?" Are you mad? If those quacks fell down the stairs in broad daylight they'd put the fault on us. I'll tell you what the regulations say, don't do it *Live* unless it's absolutely essential."

"What are we going to do?"

"We? It's your problem!" Fred feigned a gentle soothing tone and tilted his head. "Northover, I know it's a big responsibility but I cannot do everything. Just make sure you don't do the job *Live*."

"Thanks! I can't switch the power off, and I can't do it live."

"I know I can trust you to find a way."

Northover stared at Fred with contempt. "Have you tried getting doctors, nurses and administration staff, all to agree the same time? Admin are breathing down my neck and the November nights are making residents nervous."

"Out!" snapped Fred. "But remember, a hospital never shuts!"

Northover replaced the Health & Safety book back on the shelf and went to make his exit, the slight bend in his back creating a tyre in his midriff. Fred called him back with a patronising air.

"Northover, what shift is Danny?"

"You should know. You approved his week's holiday."

"And who's on the residential job?"

"You suggested the new man, Charlie."

"I'm merely reminding you to use your initiative. Ah! You've brought my air freshener."

Northover left, his face burning from Fred's buck-passing. He frequently attended meetings and made excuses for him. Even took reprimands from Admin. Fred was clever making sure Danny, the Health and Safety Representative, was away and then putting the new man on the job.

He donned his bright green waterproof jacket and lolloped down towards the flats in the drizzling rain. He took a short-cut across the greenery at the rear of the hospital to avoid medical staff, his gumboots squelching through the soggy grass.

Northover could see the twelve blocks of three-storeyed flats in the distance. The first five blocks housed doctors from a host of Commonwealth countries, the remainder were taken up by nurses. Fred didn't want anything to do with them; he was an Electrical Engineer not a diplomat, he often reminded Northover

The flat concrete-roofed electric sub-station stood alone in a field east of the flats like a pillbox. He entered the windowless cell, a dank and cold place that had just two bulkhead sixty-watt fixed to the concrete walls. A haze of cement dust floated towards the open door as he entered; deposits from the drilled wall. The drilling machine lay on the floor tangled in its own lead along with the spread of Charlie's tools.

Charlie was half way up the aluminium steps, his back to Northover. He was clipping a thick armoured cable to the wall that came from the outside, an upgraded cable for the Residential. The cable needed to be bridged from wall to the prodigious electrical panel that stood in the middle of the room. The job was to connect the new cable to the heavy control panel of switches and control boxes, attached to a framework six feet high and ten feet long.

"How you doing?" asked Northover.

Charlie jerked on his steps, face white with dust, goggles blurring his vision. He took them off. "Can't you whistle? I was in deep concentration before you crept in."

Northover ignored the remark. "Is that the last of the clipping?"

"Yea. I've just got to cross over to the panel and connect up."

"Right, pack your tools. You can finish it when we have the power off."

Charlie gave him a quizzical look. "What are you talking about?"

"I've been busy lately; haven't had time to circulate memos about the shut-down."

"What do you expect me to do? I'm half a day ahead on this little number."

"That oil sump job has been hanging around for weeks."

"Sump pump!" Blurted Charlie. "That's bloody punishment posting. I've worked my guts out on this job to have an hour to myself."

"I cannot allow the power to be off for an hour without giving notice."

"An hour? Ten minutes, once I've stripped and glanded the cable-ends."

"The fact that power will be disrupted will come back on me."

"I'll drill the casing Live, then switch off. Ten minutes to connect, that's all. Vandals cause bigger supply cuts than that."

"I wouldn't drill the bus-bar chamber Live, Charlie."

"You wouldn't! You came from University straight into the office. I've had a bit more practical experience."

"I can't authorise Live working conditions."

"Just leave me for the rest of the day. I'll cover your butt for you."

Northover left, happy he got the message to Charlie without

compromising himself.

Charlie set about finalising the job, thinking how Northover would get the credit. He opened up the rectangular bus-bar panel and carefully wedged a block of wood between the live conductors and the metal casing. The block would prevent his drill from touching the live bars. With everything at hand, it wouldn`t take long to complete the job.

He climbed his steps and drilled four quarter-inch holes in the top of the steel bus-bar casing to fix the new switch on top; the drill tip stopping half an inch from the wooden block. Before he could fix it, a bigger hole was needed to cater for the entry of the thick cable. Inserting a four-inch circular cutter in the hand drill, he began boring. It went well at first, the cutter screeching and chewing a shining circle into the grey metal. Drilling from the steps was more difficult with the circular cutter as it required more pressure, so he climbed to a higher tread on the steps and put his shoulder against the drill to give him extra pressure. He applied more cutting grease to help the cutter bite. The cutter began sticking and juddering, jarring his shoulder and wrist. The cutting grease began to burn and smoke, the pungency irritating his nose and stinging his eyes, the acrid smell spreading through the room. To help the drill bite more, he turned his wrists in a whirling motion and pressed harder. It helped, but more pressure was needed, so he pressed with greater force and circled the drill faster. Suddenly the drill pulled forward and got sucked into the chamber as the hole appeared. The protective piece of wood was knocked away and the cutter hit the live bar with Charlie`s hands still holding the drill. Then, as blue and yellow lights flashed all around, a deep humming began to sound in Charlie's brain like a mains transformer. Though he was shaking uncontrollably, his muscles locked and he was unable to let go. Charlie knew he was going to die. Then everything stopped as the 300 amp breaker tripped out. He felt himself being violently jerked backwards and Charlie collapsed to the floor in a black cloud. He lay on the floor trembling out of control. His muscles felt as though he had been kicked all over. His hands were burning. That wasn't too serious he had a few burns before but he couldn't see. That was worrying him. That was bad. He hadn't experienced blindness. He had heard of people having temporary blindness after a flash. It only lasted ten minutes. It lasted longer with Charlie. He waited and waited until Northover came after a complaint from several doctors that they had no power in their flats. He found Charlie staring, still waiting for daylight to penetrate his eyes.

* * *

Well?" demanded Fred, as Northover walked into his office.

Three weeks had slowly past. Northover had been given the job of escorting the Health & Safety Inspector to the scene of the accident. It had taken that long because Charlie didn't have his sight back for three days. Then he'd had two weeks on the sick. Now that he was back in work he had to face the Inspector and the consequences of an inquiry.

"It's all right," said Northover. "Charlie admitted it was his fault. He got off with a warning. He was told if he did it again he could face a fine of £1000 and/or three months imprisonment."

"He's a lucky man. He should have known the H&S Regs" state that each man is responsible for his own safety and of others. Has the Inspector gone? Danny's in this afternoon, isn't he?"

"Three o'clock. I suppose I should have told him the Inspector was coming this morning, but I forgot completely."

"I had an internal letter off Admin". They're very pleased with the new lighting down the Residential area."

"Wonderful. I'm glad somebody's happy."

"Has that job on the sump pump been done yet?"

"I'll put Danny on it this afternoon. It will keep him occupied for a few hours."

The Cycle

The Birth of the raindrop is lonely
until nursed in a mountain stream,
where it jinks along in the
pastures of youth
unmindful of where it has been.

Trained into the river of awe,
trapped in laborious lake,
exalted in wine, abused in sewers,
redundant in factory waste.

Destined for the aged estuary,
spewed into the sea of death,
it stops, no further to go,
like a dying man on his last breath.

Up rises Hope, The Sun of Life,
and the Spirit of Vapour decrees,
wherever the raindrop is lost in the ocean,
it shall be lifted, cleansed and set free.

Tragic but True

She lay there in the subdued light, too weak to move, and whispered as loud as she could. "Billy, Billy, please turn me, son. The pain is getting worse on this side."

Billy gently pushed his hands underneath the frail body of his mother but could not gain enough of her to turn her. The once full-figured woman had lost her stoutness, her muscles worn, her face hollow, and her skin loose. Through her thin nightdress, he could feel her flesh folding under the pressure of his sliding hands. He pressed down into the mattress, tunnelling his hands around her body, disturbing a mixture of medical smells and odours of incontinence.

"Can I help?" asked his younger sister, Ann, sitting the other side of the single bed.

"No, I know how to do it now. Ready, Mam? Here we go."

He lifted and rolled her, pulling her to him as he did it. She cried out, then whispered her ghostly gratitude. "Thank you, Billy."

"Is that better?"

"Yes, thank you."

In minutes, she was in a shallow sleep, fighting the pains of her body, her low rhythmic moans illustrating her suffering. It was a respite that prevailed until the acuteness of her agony erupted and she would cry out to be turned again.

Billy looked across the bed to his sister. He had never been so miserable. The sadness on his sister's face returned the same feeling.

"Is there anything else we can do?" she said softly.

He shook his head, not daring to speak his mind. What he had to say was not for his mother's ears. He wanted to tell his sister it was all too late. That all that exercise they had helped their mother through had been futile. The gentle chastising when she dragged her feet and wanted to give up, sandwiched between them, had all been a con. The drives in the country, spooning the Complan into her, squeezing the orange segments on her dry lips was all useless. The surgeon was a liar who thought little people like them couldn't face the truth. "What shall we do?" his older sister had asked the surgeon. "We're a big family and can take it in turns to do whatever is necessary to make her better." The surgeon had replied so convincingly, "Plenty of fresh air, gentle exercise, give her to eat whatever she wants and she'll be fine."—The condescending liar!

His sister was aware of the anger in his face. "Billy, are you all right? Shall I make a cup of tea? If we're to stay awake all night We'll need to keep eating and drinking."

"I'll make it. It will take my mind off things."

When he had gone, she looked at her mother. The change on her body and face was indecent, and it only took three months. Three months to turn a smiling full-faced lady into a...into a skeleton almost. She turned away and buried her head in her hands. How could they have missed it? Six years she had been cleared. Six years after being trussed up like an animal having radium treatment. "It's embarrassing," her Mam had told her. "I Don't want to go through that again." Not once did they suspect—"Infiltration of the bowels." That was the medical term. What a nice technical name they gave it. And Mam, being too proud to have her constipation seen to, decided to take senapodes. Senapodes! And all the time that grotesque...haggis...was growing on the side of her stomach. Yes, that's what it looked like, a haggis growing on her side.

Billy popped his head around the door. "Are you coming in the kitchen for it? We'll be able to hear her. It's all right."

In the kitchen, she took off her glasses and wiped her eyes with a paper handkerchief.

"It's not fair. She's raised her children and baby-sat her grandchildren. Now she has time to enjoy herself she's cut down without any reward. First Dad and now her, it's not fair, Billy."

"Yesterday she asked me to go up to the mountain spring," sighed Billy. "She wanted me to bring back a bottle of its water. It might do the trick she said. I got a bottle of it for her. She enjoyed a few sips."

"Are you going to go down to the Hospital Administrator again?"

"No point. I gave him a good rollicking a week ago. The best he could do was to send that surgeon, who done the job, up to see her."

"Yes. And what did he say as soon as he came in. "What are they doing to you, Mrs Morgan?" As though we were at fault for her condition."

"Arrogant swine! We would never have found out had he not gone on holiday."

"At least his registrar was truthful."

"Aye, he didn't give us a load of fiction. I could have coped with her dying, but why tell us she was going to be all right? Me and David held her by her arms when she was trying to walk. Two massive operations and he tells us to feed her up and exercise her. Arrogant idiot!"

"Not so loud, Mam might hear you."

Billy finished his tea and looked out at the darkness through the rear window. Occasionally the moon broke through and brightened the garden. Then a black cloud came over and it was heavy and dismal again. Just like his spirit had been. Good news, tragic news.

"That black doctor was right, you know."

"What black doctor?"

"The locum for Doctor Williamson; the one Marion went to see and quarrelled with when he told her Mam had three months to live. The one none of us believed. It was easier to believe the load of lies the surgeon told us."

"Marion said he refused Mam a specialist."

"Numbers aren't we? Wasting the specialist's time and costing unnecessary expense and suffering, he told her. And her going crazy trying to get Mam into hospital."

"It's a good job doctor Williamson returned from holiday. Mam would never had been admitted."

"He should have examined her. He couldn't be bothered either. I'm going back into her."

They sat either side of the bed again, just looking at her, listening to her shallow breathing and quiet moans. What could they do? It was a matter of waiting for her last breaths. They'd seen death before. Their father had passed away three years ago. They had understood his passing. He was a man who had been warned to cut out drinking, cut out smoking, eat this food, eat that food. But he didn't, so his death was painful but understandable. But their mother was clean-living, meek and mild; having a few years of happiness before old age. Sixty six and she had looked as if she could go another twenty years.

She cried out in pain.

"What can I do Mam?" asked Ann. "Tell me and I'll do it."

"Billy, turn me, boy," she whispered "It'll ease the pain. Turn me, son."

He went through the process again, trying his best to be as gentle as possible. But even though his mother was stones lighter, her awkward position made it difficult. She tried to scream, but had not the strength, her sound was like the wailing of a wind on the chimney. Then she sank into a deep moan which couldn't be controlled.

"They made us take her down to the hospital for a bloody check-up," Billy said in a sharp whisper. "Me and Marion had to carry her in, almost. People offered their seats because she couldn't stand. And when we sat her down we had to support her. And all the time they knew she was not fit enough to do all that."

"I know. Marion told me."

"We waited so long I had to go to the office and demand to see the matron. They moved then. I made such a fuss the crafty swine wouldn't let us in to see the registrar until they had two nurses as witnesses."

"I know, Billy. Let it go."

"I can't let it go. And then the registrar asked would I leave so that he could examine Mam. Up until then we thought she was going to be all right."

"I know. When Marion came out, she told you that the registrar couldn't understand why Mam was made to go there for a check-up. He told Marion she was a dying woman. The cancer had gone too far."

Billy buried his head in his hands.

"She had to stop you going back into him, didn't she?"

"As soon as we got Mam home, I went back down. The Administrator was very apologetic and promised an enquiry. Huh!"

An agonising intake of breath erupted from their mother. "Billy, turn me, please. Billy?"

"I'm here, Mam. Hang on. Are you ready? Here we go."

She settled, gave three diminishing breaths, and went silent.

Billy looked at her motionless body. "Mam?"

Ann stared for seconds looking shocked. Then she went into her bag and brought out a hand mirror. She put it to her mother's nostrils. There was no breath.

The Doubtful Conscript

Oh Lord I've tried to follow You,
I sing your hymns and psalms.
I read your words penned by the Saints
but something's very wrong.
The ways of man are different,
I do not understand,
they've taken me from passive life
and thrust a rifle in my hand.
The family you created
is spread across the seas,
they are my kin and we agree,
to and love live in peace.
Your spirit fed me wholesome faith,
and made my life complete,
If I should kill as war demands,
will my brother's corpse lie at my feet?

You gave me strength to face life's trials
and I shall carry on,
though I wear a uniform
I still know right from wrong.
Those who shone with veneered grace
when I was naïve and young
are preaching patriotism
and favouring bombs and guns.
You taught me to discern
who is friend or foe
and I shall know my enemies
when they break down by door

It's then I'll fight until I die
to save my waiting soul.
Then You
shall judge,
and I shall pray
that You will call me home.

Delicate Time

It was a warm sunny day as Dawn took her young child for a walk in its pram. "Hello Mrs Price!" she called, seeing her neighbour strolling in the park. Dawn sauntered through the park gates pushing the pram, her sleeping infant oblivious to the world. "I've been meaning to call on you but I just didn't know what to say. How is your husband now?" She quickened her step and caught up with Mrs Price.

"He's not too bad, thanks," said the seventy-one-year-old, her voice quiet and cordial. "Don't ask me what it's all about. He's always been a mystery to me."

Dawn smiled at her last remark. "You've been with him long enough to know how his brain ticks."

"Forty five years and he's still a cryptic clue to me."

"It's good to see you out and about, anyway."

"It's such a nice day I thought I'd take in some fresh air in the park."

"The park always looks beautiful in the Spring. Helps take your mind off things."

The elderly lady and the young mother ambled up the gradient to the castle. Children were screaming and laughing in the play area, and there was a refreshing fragrance drifting down the road from the flower beds.

"I knew there was something wrong," said Mrs Price, her thin face lined and tired. "He had been moody for weeks. He's been a moody man all his life, but when he got involved in nostalgia he cheered up for some time. Nostalgia is not for me, soaps are more to my liking."

"I like watching the soaps, too. It takes you out of yourself."

Mrs Price nodded in a cursory fashion, eager to talk, so Dawn let her. "He had his records and I had my TV so I thought things were all right. But then a few months ago he changed for the worse and became quiet and worried-looking. He'd rush to the door when he saw the postman approaching as though he expected a cheque from the Pools."

"I saw him on the doorstep a couple of times looking up and down the road."

Waiting for the postman I have no doubt. I questioned him about it but he told me not to worry. "Nothing for you to worry your head over," he'd say. I dare not probe, it would make him worse, though it got me thinking he might be carrying on and got some dreadful floozy."

Dawn giggled. "They do go funny in old age, they say."

"It's not funny, Dawn."

"Sorry. He walked past me the other day as though he didn't know me."

"I know. He's terrible. People come on to me in the street and ask me if they have offended him."

"I think I would have panicked under those circumstances."

"He sits there deep in thought, but if the telephone rings he's out of his starting blocks like Lynford Christie."

"Somebody telephoned him, did you say?"

"I don't know. But he seems relieved when the calls are for me. Strange man my husband. I`m glad for the fresh air."

Reaching the benches in front of the castle, they sat, the sun warm on their faces, the birds flying to the budding trees in the woods. The young mother checked on the sleeping baby then sighed.

"How old is she now, Dawn?"

Dawn shook her blonde hair back over her shoulders, a contented expression on her round healthy face. "Fourteen months, two weeks and three days."

"She's beautiful. You must be very proud of her."

"I love her to bits."

Mrs Price smiled and sat back, grateful for the cordial spring day and the soft breeze carrying the distant sounds of the children in the play area. But then an inner breeze blew images across her mind; images that admonished her for not taking more interest in her husband.

"He bought a four hundred pound music stereo, you know. I told him, I hope you've paid down for that. We've never been in debt in our lives, and we're not starting now. Then he bought CDs. They're not cheap. Bought some locally, others he sent away for. The discs took him back to our teenage days. He used to sit in his room when I was cleaning and he'd call me. "Come and listen to this," he'd say. "We used to dance to this music in the Palace accompanied by real bands; saxophones, trumpets, double bass. Not like the canned rubbish they have these days." I'd stop and listen and nod and smile just to humour him."

"Well, you did what you could."

"But he doesn't play them anymore, you see. That's strange. Maybe I should sit down with him and be more attentive."

"You should both take a holiday. Go abroad and get some enjoyment."

"Waste of money. We Don't waste money. I tell him: I hope you're getting your money's worth out of those records! They cost enough."

"Well, it's his hobby, I suppose."

Mrs Price shook her head. "I just wish I knew why he changed so suddenly after being so content with his music. I wish I knew what he expected through the post, or who might have been on the telephone. He's always been deep. Can't get a word out of him at times."

"It will all come out one day. Probably nothing to worry about at all."

Dan Price was sitting in his lounge, thinking, a frown on his gaunt face. Thinking how he had been duped; imagining faceless officials behind desks studying the Fools File on a screen. How he is, at present, a number on some remote computer where they put all gullible people. Under his number was his name and assessment: Dan Price, easily intimidated, hooked, susceptible to threats, just mention the black list and he'll pay up.

Then the telephone rang and his heart thumped against his chest. He gingerly picked up the dreaded receiver.

"Hello? "Is that Mr Price?" came a sweet female voice.

He immediately became suspicious of the cajoling voice. "Speaking," he said, squinting his eyes as though the caller could see him.

"I hope I'm not disturbing you."

"You are! What is it?"

"My name is Wendy Waring. I'm calling on behalf of Nosti Discs."

A sharp intake of breath, then anger took over. "I've told you I don't want anything more to do with you. Leave me alone!"

"According to our records you haven't bought any CDs for the last three months," she said, with a delicate but patronising tone.

"That's because I didn't want your damn discs. I've written time and time again telling you I only want music from the 1950s. Each time you ignore my letters and send me another unwanted disc."

"Now, when you signed our binding contract, you signed for the whole range which was on offer at the time. That included Sixties and Seventies."

I didn't sign a contract and I don't want your discs. Can't you understand that? I answered an advert in the paper, that's all. I only wanted Fifties discs. And I don't want those anymore."

"We have a really generous offer at the moment which I'm sure you will benefit from...."

"I don't want them! Do you hear me? I paid for the last assignment because... well... because you threatened to put me on the black list. I've never been in debt in my entire life...you stupid girl...."

"There is no need to be rude, Mr Price."

"You've made me hate my Fifties songs. I can't play them because they remind me of the stress you cause me."

"What I'll do for you, Mr Price, is send you a late Sixties which is on special offer. You will receive a free Seventies CD to go with it. That's two discs for the price of one. £15.95 for *two* discs. An offer you cannot refuse."

"Are you listening there? Can you hear me? You think you've got me in your clutches but you haven't. I won't pay. Not a penny more will I give you. Don't send anymore records."

"Right, that's settled, Mr Price. I hope you'll enjoy the specially selected songs we have chosen for you and I'm sure you'll have hours of nostalgia."

"Don't ring off. I don't want your discs. Stick your discs you bitch... I'll see my solicitor...." It was then a humming came into Mr Price's brain and he felt faint.

"Please pay promptly Mr Price as it is company policy to reward prompt payers by offering them one of our Country and Western latest discs."

"What? You still there? Listen, will you please listen. I have written to you pointing out my preferences... I have written to your Box No. to your main British office and to your European Headquarters...."

"I see. Well, you'll know all about our offers. I am sure you will find our latest 60s disc and the free 70s very enjoyable. Thank you once again. By for now."

The line went dead so he slammed the phone down and lay back on the sofa. Then the silence of the room made him feel lonely and in a state of despair. The thought of Hilda finding the letter about the black list, and the gossip it would cause in the village was too stressful, so he paid for the last unwanted discs, suppressing any scandal that might have occurred, again they're pestering him. "How can I get out of it", he mumbled to himself. "Hilda mustn't know about the black list. Oh they won't do that to me, surely. Shame! Shame it will be. I won't pay for anymore," he whispered. "They're not going to get any extra money out of me." But he knew in his heart he would pay. He had contacted the office where black-listed people could verify their details and was relieved to discover his name was not on it. "I won't pay," he whispered again." Then his head buzzed and he lost consciousness and flopped back on the settee.

∗∗∗

It was a month later when Dawn and Mrs Price met in the park again. Dawn was surprised to see the lady jovial and wanting to talk. Dawn suggested they sit near the café because the young mother wanted some refreshments.

"He's sleeping much better now, you know," said Mrs Price. I was worried sick for a while. Slight stroke it was.

"Oh good, things back to normal?"

"Not at first. He was still restless at night. He wouldn't admit it, but he tossed and turned keeping me awake many times."

"But he's fine now, is he, Mrs Price?

"Yes, thank goodness

"We'll celebrate with a cup of tea."

"I shall pay for my own, love. I like to pay my way, you see. One thing about Dan and I, we owe money to nobody."

Dawn kindly brought the teas whilst Mrs Price sat at the white plastic table outside in the sunshine looking after the sleeping baby. Then they sipped at their teas. There were coins on the table which Mrs Price had placed there.

"Do you know, he came home from the pub one night, smiling and looking his usual self. I said to him, you're in a good mood all of a sudden. "Life is too short to worry about things," he said. What have you been worrying about these past six nine months? I asked him. "I haven't been worried, just a little bit down, that's all." Down? Down? You've been in a bottomless pit. I told him."

"What did he say then?"

"He told me he had been drinking with his mate, Dave, who had introduced him to a friend of his and that they had a good time talking about things. Things! Now what are things, Dawn?"

Dawn giggled. "Men's talk I expect."

"Not at their age."

Dawn nudged Mrs Price, a mischievous twinkle in her eye. "They say there's no fool like an old fool. Maybe they've been planning something."

It was Mrs Price's turn to be amused as she laughed at the insinuation. "My husband's retired, Dave is retired and their new friend of theirs is about to retire from the Trading Standards Office. They're all in love with their pint glasses."

"And he's been all right ever since that night?"

"Yes, thank goodness. Apparently, this new friend from the Trading Standards has made a strong impression on my husband."

"So life is normal again and he's back to his nostalgic records I expect?"

Mrs Price appeared perplexed for a few moments and then said. "Men are difficult to understand, Dawn, as you'll find out. I said to him the following day, I haven't heard you play your records for a while. He gave an indistinguishable grunt and went for a walk. But he's always been deep."

The Talking Salmon

Wading humbly through mating life,
not knowing why I live,
I feel the pressure of adverse currents.
But instinctively I sieve
through cloudy relentless streams,
urging me on to the spawning grounds.
I exhaust my energy jumping life's weirs.
I bruise my spirit with confusion; I fear all
my tumbling, toiling, setbacks and falls may break me to pieces
and gain nothing at all.
That phenomenon of power
driving my ambition,
forces me into an obligation
that I should make contribution
to the planet's abundant population.
It would be a pleasure to turn down stream;
to be carried along, to float, to dream.
I don't know why those starving millions
should see their young shoals die so vile.
To be conceived on dried-up rivers,
to be consumed by ant and fly.
I don't know why life needs my seed,
or if my journey will be worthwhile.
I strive along with a moral theory:
that my eggs bring forth moderate fish.
Had my kind abstained from procreation,
The world would be full of Piranhas Sharks.

Visiting Time

As he crossed the road from the workshop, combing his shock of black fuzzy hair, Danny's radio transmitter screamed intermittently. He drew it from the hip like a six-gun, pulled on the aerial with his teeth and pressed the trigger. "Danny Barr!"

A female voice, distorted by static, answered. "Lift No. 1, Danny. The alarm is sounding."

"Okay, darling."

He tucked his gold neck-chain into his open denim shirt, holding his plastic toolbox tightly under his left arm. Taking a short cut through X-ray, where a queue of grim faces gave him tired glances, he quickly arrived at the lift hall. Rows of visitors stood facing the three stainless steel doors as he watched the indicating lights bring No.1 down. The doors opened and two boys in their early teens came out grinning, and then ran yelling down the corridor.

"Flaming kids," grunted Danny.

The strident bleep sounded again. It was Mary the telephonist saying that a trainee anaesthetist had just come from theatre and wanted to use the shower outside her on-call room and that the light was not working.

Going back to the workshop for a 60 watt, his radio/transmitter bleeped again. It was Tina. No 2 lift was stuck on the third floor and there were passengers in it.

After hurrying through the corridors and up the three flights of stairs he burst into the third-floor lift hall panting, his thin face ashen. The door of No. 2 was closed. He pressed the button. The doors opened. Inside, shoulder to shoulder, pushed up against every side of the lift, were twelve people. Some smiled at him, some stared. A middle-aged lady told him there was no room.

"You've triggered the overload switch," he said. "Four of you will have to get out," but the doors closed automatically. He pressed the button again opening the door, the crowd still sardined and perplexed. He held his hand on the button preventing the doors closing.

Slowly, but reluctantly an attractive lady got out, then a man and a young couple. The doors closed and the lift moved off.

"Damn lifts are useless," the man said, and walked away to the stairs accompanied by the young couple. The attractive lady waited, then shook, startled at the strident sound of Danny's bleep sounding yet again.

He smiled at her, drew his RT from his hip and pulled the aerial, looking deep into her eyes. "Danny Barr."

The sound of visitors chatter, plus a porter pushing a squeaky hot-lock full of rattling dirty crockery through the lift hall, convinced him he'd better pick up an internal phone on the near wall. He dialled switchboard. "Danny here."

"It's me, Mary. The anaesthetist has been on to me again. She's still waiting for a shower."

"I haven't picked up my loofah yet."

"Don't be facetious, Danny. She's a bit upset. I told her you had an urgent job but she demands her light be fixed."

"Demands, does she? I carry most things in my toolbox, but bulbs and fluorescent tubes won't fit."

"I've got to pass the message on."

Okay Mary, darling. Keep the kettle warm."

On his return journey from the workshop his bleep went off. "Danny here."

"Short Stay requires your presence, Danny," said Tina. "They need to use their liquidiser urgently, but it hasn't got a plug it."

"Okay." The call sounded more urgent than the shower bulb so he made his way to Short Stay Ward. At the corridor junction, a domestic pushed her scrubber-polisher at him. "Where's my table lamp, Danny?" He jumped over her machine. "Haven't had time. Don't worry I'll do it."

The Sister in Short Stay stood at the nurses' station, a dumpy woman whose ample chest stretched her navy uniform to the limit. She was peeling surgical gloves off her hands. A pungent smell of ointment rose from them.

Danny screwed his face up. "Good god. What's that smell?"

"Embrocation. Want some?" Danny backed off as she pushed the gloves near his nose, then she disposed of them in a bin. "Do me a favour, Danny."

"Is it urgent? I've got an anaesthetist on my back."

"Turn around. It's all right, boy, she's gone. Listen. I have a mentally handicapped little girl in the single ward there." She pointed to the room opposite her station. "Besides her obvious problems she's been brought in because she has a virus. Now, she's physically incapable of eating solids." She pointed to a cardboard box on the floor. "I managed to dig out a liquidiser from our store room, but it has no plug on it."

Using the nursing station as a bench he realised the liquidiser had a break in its lead near the entry. "I'll have to dismantle it. The plug's been removed by maintenance because the lead is faulty. It needs repairing."

The demure mother of the little girl came out of the cubicle. "I'm so sorry to be of trouble. It's my fault. I should have brought a liquidiser with me but everything happened so quickly."
Danny sympathised with her. Her face, having no make-up, was drained, tired and worn, her sandy hair lifeless and greying.

"Don't you worry, my love, ten minutes and We'll have it fixed." Danny looked at the Sister. "Can I go into your Prep" Room? There's more space."

"By all means," said Sister, swinging her arms, ham-acting. "The ward is yours, just get it fixed."

The mother felt guilty. "Sister, I Don't live far from here. I could go and get mine," she said.

"No, no. You go back into little Wendy. Danny won't be long."

He took the liquidiser apart, cut off the offending piece of flex, and reconnected it. Then his RT bleeped.

The ward Sister jumped from her chair. "Good god Danny, that thing will wake the mortuary guests."

He picked up the phone on the nursing station. "Danny Barr."

Mary apologised. "It's the anaesthetist again. She's furious. She said if you Don't put a bulb in her shower immediately she's going to report you to the on-call Administrator."

"I'm on an emergency in Short Stay, she'll have to wait."

"She also said she's going to write a letter to your supervisor to have you disciplined."

Danny smirked, "She don't know what she's talking about. Bye."

Just as he was completing the repair of the liquidiser, his RT sounded yet again.

"That bleeper is ridiculous, " said the Sister, putting her fingers to her ears.

Danny picked up the phone again. "Mary? Now listen—I'm"

"It's No. 3 Danny. It's stuck between the 3rd and 4th. The passengers are panicking."

"Get in touch with the plant attendant. Tell him I'll bring it to the third floor, Sorry Sister. Visitors stuck in the lift."

The Sister looked at the mother "What can one do, Mrs Thomas?"

Opening the door of the roof-top control room, a blast of noise hammered his ear-drums as roaring generators, motors, contacts, flywheels and screeching brakes made a thunderous din. A thin haze of electric-blue smoke gave the room a sharp smell of heated electrics. After manually bringing the lift to the 3rd. floor, he made his way down.

Dave, the plant attendant, was talking through the closed door of the lift assuring the passengers. A student nurse and a domestic assistant were waiting there, determined to see the drama to its conclusion.

"Won't be long now folks," said Dave. Seeing Danny come with his thumb up, Dave slotted his long V-shaped key into the V-hole in the door and pulled the doors open. Three women and two men emerged, one of the ladies, on the point of collapse, being aided by her husband. "Will someone get a chair for my wife?" he asked. The domestic obliged and the nurse went for water.

Danny returned to the Short Stay unit and finally completed the repair to the liquidiser. He was about to test it when his RT bleeped.

"You should throw that in a bucket of water," the Sister suggested.

"Danny here."

"Pick up an outside phone, please," said Mary. "Sorry Danny. It's William, the on-call Administrator"

He picked up the phone on the nursing station. "Hello?"

"Danny?"

"How are you, William?"

"I'm fine. Danny, I've been contacted by an anaesthetist who complained most bitterly about you refusing to renew her bulb in her shower. Surely not!"

"Of course not, I'm repairing a liquidiser for a child who is physically unable to eat solids; I'm also having trouble with the lifts; it is visiting time, you know. I'm up and down the stairwell like a bungee jumper, but if you think I should drop everything and.."

"No, no Danny. I get the picture. Make it your first non-priority job, will you?"

"If luck holds it will be done in the next five minutes."

"Thank you Danny. I'll leave it up to you."

After renewing the bulb in the shower room, he knocked on the on-call room door, wanting to let the anaesthetist know the job had been done, but got no answer. He knocked again then gave up.

At the switchboard, he threw his toolbox in the rest room and slumped on a chair in front of the control board. Calling lights lit up and the girls were busy plugging in and answering the calls. A stale smell of cigarettes reminded him he hadn't had one for a time.

"The shower-light done, Danny?" asked Mary, her headphones pulling on her short brown hair as she turned round.

"All done. Now that the visitors are settled we should have an hour's peace. How about a cup of tea?" He lit a cigarette.

"I've boiled the kettle. Take over a minute Tina," she said to her colleague, I need a break. She went into the adjoining rest room and came back with a cup of tea and a half eaten packet of biscuits.

The first sip hit him hotly at the back of the throat. "Ah that's great." He took a drag from his cigarette to keep the feeling there. "I'm going to have ten minutes before I start on my maintenance."

"Yea. There'll be a lull on the board shortly." Though Tina was busy plugging and unplugging.

They heard footsteps coming through the rest room which connected with outer corridor. A female doctor in a white working coat walked in and stood at the door. "I am not going to tolerate it any longer. I want the name of the technician," she snorted.

Danny felt the venom in her sharp voice. He looked up at her. She was beautiful, young and shapely but he wasn't too keen on her hair tied up in a bun. He could see her brown eyes were full of fire. "That's me. Daniel Barr," he said. "Pleased to meet you."

She looked down at him. "I'm not pleased to meet you! I have been waiting ages for a light in my shower while you sit there smoking and drinking tea."

"It's all done and tested. Sorry but I've been busy on urgent jobs, couldn't get round to it."

"Don't lie to me. I've just come from there. It is not fixed."

The telephonists turned from their boards, wondering if an

awkward scene was about to develop.

Danny's jovial disposition deserted him for a moment. "I renewed the bulb just five minutes ago."

She stared at him, thinking. "You renewed it because I reported you to the Administrator."

"Your light is fixed, doctor I can do no more." He picked a biscuit from the packet and sipped his tea. He looked at the switchboard. "There are four lights up girls." They turned to the switchboard and answered the calls. The anaesthetist stood there for few seconds staring at him. "You should be sacked!" Then she turned and left insisting he had not heard the last of the incident.

I'm sorry," said Mary. "I couldn't pacify her."

Danny shook his head, nibbling at his biscuit. "No problem. A bit more experience and she'll understand. We'll all be here when the trainees have matured and left."

Remembrance

Valiant people:
Grocers, bakers, sons and daughters,
wrenched from loving homes
they learned to hate and fight.
Solicitors, teachers, mothers, fathers,
their eyes were closed
to give us freedom's light.

Headless bodies, limbless torsos,
bloodless veins, emptied tubes,
eyeless sockets, tortured souls,
disintegration of unknown braves.

Through the liberty of November morning
we march grim-faced, stiff-lipped, proud.
Brandishing medals, flags,
wreaths and uniforms -
do we see dead faces now?

Ambiguous eyes fill with memories,
uncertain hearts drum self-esteem.
We are saved and reap the glory,
they are gone no more to dream.
Could we deign one day a year
to stand naked at the cenotaph,
we`d prove beyond the doubting graves
we honour them and not ourselves.

Old Mates

As he made his way to his favourite beauty spot along the open country road, Douglas breathed in deeply. The freshness of the gently breeze filled his lungs and a sense of freedom lifted his heart. The retired office worker had only one negative thought; it was his old colleague Cledwyn. He hoped Cledwyn would not turn up today, but immediately he felt guilty. If he should turn up I will try hard to be patient with him, he thought. Yes, I must be more tolerant with Cledwyn. His conscience clear, he felt his spirit lifting as he left the black and white of the industrial town to the colourful brilliance of the verdant landscape. He'd had dark thoughts of Cledwyn, but he'd cast them aside and admonish himself for not being tolerant. He was going to be pleasant and polite if Cledwyn should turn up. He would not allow Cledwyn to provoke him today. Why am I thinking of Cledwyn? He mumbled to himself.

He turned round the bend and looked down the valley where the hazel trees flanked the green slopes and the Taff Fechan River flowed slowly through. No, the retired sixty two year-old office worker was not going to allow his egotistical old mate to spoil his day however much he provoked him. The subject of his retired pastime which had become the love of his life would not be mentioned if at all possible.

At the bottom of the tree-lined winding road he reached a Y junction, chose the right-hand lane and walked up the gradient to the Mountain Railway. He bought a cup of tea from the little café (several converted arched-roofed goods vans, painted brown and cream) and went outside to sit on the nearest picnic bench. From the elevated spot he marveled at the panoramic view. Below, shimmering in the gentle breeze, curving around the valley and flanked by the wooded hillsides, was Ponsticill Reservoir reflecting the blue sky. In the distance the three pale-green peaks of the Brecon Beacons gave a mountainous natural backdrop. Douglas sighed contentedly savouring the vista of the beauty spot.

Hearing the whistle of the train coming down the line he looked behind in time to see the maroon train emerge from the trees a little way up the track. The steam panted from its funnel pulling its wooden carriages as it rumbled through the small station. Children waved enthusiastically from its windows as it tooted, before disappearing down the line into the hazel woods. It left the tranquil place in silence. But then he heard the crunch of gravel behind him and a familiar baritone voice boomed out:

"Douglas, I had a feeling you might be here."

Douglas could not help his five feet, six-inch figure wriggle with irritation. "You know I'm here every Wednesday, weather permitting," he said, caressing his bald head, nervously.

"It's a lovely day, Douglas."

"It is indeed, Cledwyn."

Cledwyn maneuvered his large frame around the picnic bench dragging his left leg and sat side-saddle opposite Douglas. His podgy fingers curled round the rim of Douglas's polystyrene cup of tea and moved it aside. He lifted his mates hand shaking it vigorously as he always did with regular annoyance. "How are you today Douglas?"

Douglas nodded, tugged his hand from Cledwyn's vice and recovered his cup. He looked at his stocky companion and could only admire his healthy physic; though he was ten years older than Douglas, his shock of grey hair, square features and six-foot stature showed a man looking younger than his age. "I'm fine Cledwyn, how are you?"

"Couldn't be better except for my gammy knees, but you Don't look too good to me; you look a bit peaky, man."

"There's nothing wrong with me. How are your knees, anyway?"

"Still the same; too much jarring of the patellae in youthful events."

"Yes, you have mentioned it," said Douglas, reminding Cledwyn he had told of his cycling achievements time and time again.

"How is the writing coming along, Douglas? Have you learnt anything from my previous advice?"

Douglas sighed. In his heart, he knew he couldn't avoid the subject of his new-found love, Creative Writing, but thought it might take a little time before Cledwyn mentioned it. "I hope you're not going to start that again."

"You mustn't be too proud to take advice, Douglas."

"I'm not too proud, it's just that I'd rather take advice from a professional tutor. What you should understand, Cledwyn, is that you

Don't know as much as you think you do."

"I could teach you a few more well-chosen words; quote a few metaphors etcetera. Tell me, do you know the difference between a metaphor and a simile?"

"Of course I do!" Douglas snapped, but closed his eyes and composed himself. "It's an elementary lesson, Cledwyn. You learn such things in primary school."

"Oh!" exclaimed Cledwyn, piqued at being accused of asking a simple question. "Right then, Let's see how far you can go."

"Cledwyn, I Don't need to go anywhere, I'm enjoying the peace of the country and the beauty of the surrounding view. You have this obsession for knocking people down at every opportunity. Why Don't we just enjoy the tranquility of the surroundings."

"It's good for your soul to be humbled now and again."

"Your soul is wanting then...sorry, didn't mean that."

"Don't be so sullen; conversation is good for the brain."

"Only when it stimulates the brain but not when it dulls it." Then Douglas felt guilty. "Okay, so you`ve been at the dictionary again."

"No, no, just those words that comes to mind. Being a writer you should be able to tell me the answer to these elementary questions," he said, looking down at his hands. "Tell me, what is the meaning of charade?"

Douglas rolled his eyes and sipped his tea, his hand beginning to shake, but he knew he'd have to give an answer. "It's...well it has two meanings really...."

"You're stalling. One meaning only, I'm afraid."

"It's a kind of acting to give someone a clue, a game, and also something silly, absurd; very much like the present situation."

Cledwyn ignored his friend's rudeness and looked down again, shaking his head. "I'll give you that one. Assonance?"

"Cled, why don't you go and have a cup of tea. I was enjoying myself."

"Come on now. If you Don't know, say so." he urged.

Douglas sometimes got assonance and alliteration confused and would look it up, but today he felt he must assert himself show confidence. "I believe that is a repetition of words that have the same vowel sounds."

"Give me an example."

"No! Now change the subject you're boring me…I mean, I'm not in the mood"

"Ha! Now tell me what an anachronism is."

"You know what it means."

"I want to know if you know."

Douglas began to wish he hadn't taken up writing since his retirement; it was a subject that was giving Cledwyn more pleasure than himself. "I know it, I just can't bring it to mind."

"Rubbish! An excuse! I'll tell you what it means."

"I thought you might. If you give me time I'll search my mind."

Cledwyn shook his head and pursed his lips, "That's not good enough. As a writer you need a sharp mind."

"Tell me, Cledwyn, what words did you ask me last week and the week before and the week before that and any other opportunity that came along in the past year?"

"That's negative thinking," retorted Cledwyn, with a cool wave of his arm dismissively. Being a writer you should know those words. You need a clear and acute mind. A large vocabulary should be at your command."

Douglas looked down at the tranquil lake. "I'm going to buy a boat; that lake looks exclusive at the moment."

Cledwyn gazed into the air at nothing in particular. "I'm not a writer so it's not important for me to remember words. I'm of the opinion You've never heard of anachronism. I'll tell you what I'll do, I'll go and get a cup of tea in the cafe and when I come back I'll tell you the meaning" As he struggled to his feet he looked down at Douglas with satisfaction, his cold grey eyes mocking the watery blue of his mate's. "Yes, I think I've got you, Douglas. Never mind, I'll enlighten you when I return."

Douglas was glad of the reprieve and wondered would it be an appropriate time to leave. He decided it wasn't. His life wouldn't be worth living if he should run. Cledwyn would always be triumphant, and such a victory would not be forgotten at any social gathering the pair might be invited to. He knew Cledwyn used his loud voice to advantage, and always had order when he was about to humiliate someone, whether it be telling some old lady her shoes didn't suit her dress, or telling someone he didn't think his girlfriend was all that pretty. His remarks were always said with a joking tone which the receiver of the insult would give him the benefit of the doubt, but his words still stung. In the past Douglas tried hard to avoid his little game, for each humiliation was another penetrating sound from the constant dripping tap that resounded in his head. No, he would have to ponder awhile. But the more he thought about it the more his brain blanked out. He was annoyed with himself for allowing Cledwyn to suck him in to his egotistical sport. If only he had the courage to tell him what he really thought of him.

He decided to give his brain a rest, but he failed, so he looked around the little station which was themed on the 50s. The brown and cream railway-wagon café took him back to his teens when his mother used to take the family to the countryside for a picnic. The carriages they sat in were exactly the same colour. He remembered the giant water tower, just like the one he eyed across the track now. Then his eyes turned to the original signal box. Though not functioning, it was brown and cream and had the British Rail logo on it. It was no good. Cledwyn was in his brain blanking out all thought as always. It all began when Douglas was a young man and had started his accountant's job at the same factory known locally as the Button Factory, but officially was called Welsh Products. Cledwyn, the old hand, had taken him under his wing and ushered him to every office, store and workshop relevant to his job, making them good friends and always dining together in the works canteen. But even now at seventy two, Cledwyn couldn't let go. Douglas smiled, comparing Cledwyn to the factory stores.

Inside the café Cledwyn leaned on the small counter that partitioned the kitchen from the tables and chairs of the sitting area. There was nobody else there except the young girl behind the counter.

"Be with you in a minute," she said, as she prepared sandwiches and pastries for the expected return of the train. "The train will be back in a few minutes."

"Ah, but I have priority," he said, sounding playfully astounded. "I'm first in the queue."

The girl, acquainted with Cledwyn's teasing, turned to him. "I'll get you a cup of tea," she said.

"How do you know I want tea? I might want a lemonade or coffee."

"You always have tea."

"But I might want something different today."

She placed her hands on her hips, stooped a little and stared at him. "What do you want?"

An intense concentration spread over his face as he touched his puckered lips with his index finger and then said, "I think I'll have a cup of tea."

"Right! One tea coming up."

"I reckon it's time you changed your apron."

She scowled at him. "It's clean on this morning."

But it's lost its whiteness."

"It's cream, Cledwyn. Cream!"

As she put a tea bag in the polystyrene cup, Cledwyn looked at the small kitchen. "I hope you're aware of hygiene in this place; very important. I'm very fussy with my food."

"You said that last week, Cledwyn. You'll have to find something else to find fault with," she said, as she placed his cup of tea on the counter. "75p please."

"75p?"

"You said that last week as well. I told you then it had gone up 5p."

Cledwyn pursed his lips at her: "I've got a good mind not to buy it."

"Sugar is over on that table," she said, pointing."

"And I told you last week I Don't take sugar in my tea. You should remember your customers' tastes. Very important to make your customer feel at home."

"Yes, yes, alright, Cledwyn, I'll try and remember. Bye Cledwyn, off you go."

Cledwyn gave her a raucous laugh of satisfaction.

Douglas's mind was travelling in the past when Cledwyn emerged, rocking his way back, trying his best to protect his dry painful kneecaps and also prevent the cup from spilling. He placed his cup on the picnic table and, with difficulty, sat down.

"Well?" he asked, sharply. "You've had plenty of time to think."

Douglas puffed, "Do we have to play this childish game?"

"You're a defeatist. Shall I tell you the meaning?"

"It will come to me eventually."

"Writing will never come to you; you haven't the vocabulary. How you managed a degree I'll never know."

"My degree was in accountancy not creative writing!" he snapped. "I took up creative writing as a therapeutic and enjoyable pastime; You've put a stop to that! Besides, what have you done pumping bicycle peddles all your life? You've ended up half crippled!"

"I've rode through the country and seen the land. What about you with your fuddled brain blowing your grey matter studying? You don't even know what an anachronism is."

"I've forgotten."

"Be honest, Douglas, you haven't got a clue."

Douglas felt his blood begin to race around his veins. He was searching his brain to find something more offensive but then realised he was falling into the usual trap. He turned his head away towards the signal box trying to ignore Cledwyn's eyes and the tap of his hand on his. Douglas stared at the railway logo prominent on the woodwork and it struck him. The logo didn't belong there; it didn't fit in with the period. It was once called GWR. He smiled at his tormentor.

"If you must be such a prig, I'll tell you."

Cledwyn's eyes widened at the accusation, "I'm only trying to help you. Well?"

"An anachronism is something which is placed in the wrong period. For example, if I were writing about the 50s and I used a mobile phone in my writing, that would be an anachronism, for the mobile doesn't belong in that period."

The smile left Cledwyn's face and he conceded. "Yes, well, that explanation will do," he said, looking down. "Actually, it is a thing appropriate to a period other than that in which it exists."

"Is that how it reads in the dictionary? Douglas quipped curtly, wanting redress. "Now shall I ask you the meaning of a word? Or maybe you'd like a short story I just thought up?"

"I hope I haven't rubbed you up the wrong way," said Cledwyn. Then he leaned his elbows on the table, goading Douglas, "You're not capable of making up a short story just like that."

"I'm a writer, aren't I? I was thinking of you when you were getting your tea and a story came to mind."

"Inspired by me? Carry on, I may find an anachronism in it."

"Right, I will, that's if you have the courtesy to listen."

"Just get on with it, Douglas, lad."

"As you know I worked as an accountant in the factory before I took retirement…."

"Yes, I thought you might mention your elevated position, and I was a lowly machinist. But fortunately for you I knew the place back to front."

"You've never let me forget it."

"Furthermore," quipped Cledwyn, "I was fit and healthy. Not a pasty face stuck in a claustrophobic office."

"What your position was is nothing to do with it," grunted Douglas. "Anyway, the factory had two main stores, one small plant and one much larger plant."

"I hope your written work is more exciting than this," Douglas.

"Give me a chance, there's a moral to the tale. Anyway, because store at number No 1 was small, only a couple of hundred tools and components were kept there. And when the store man was asked for something, he could put his hand on it within seconds."

"I did work there, you know."

"Of course," continued Douglas. "However, when the store man had a large delivery, he had to leave some of his stock outside his stores because of the small capacity of his place. But as you also know, down at Plant 2, where you operated the Cincinnati.. "

"I loved that machine. I looked after it as though it were my bike."

"To continue, where you operated your baby, there was a huge machine shop that housed a hundred machines, all of which needed spare parts. There was also the main substation, a big boiler house, the laboratory, office block, a huge maintenance department…."

"I know, I know, it was a big place."

"Well, you can imagine the number of spares that had to be kept in that store. And do you know, when people went to that big store and requisitioned something, the store man would look at them for a minute or two…"

"Barry-the-stores. I remember him. He'd stick his head in the air and shout, "Ha, book C". Then he'd find book C and turn its pages over, run his finger down the page, call out the bin number, the pigeon hole number and then disappear into the maze of steel storage cabinets and return a couple of minutes later with the component."

"Are you going to let me finish?"

"He wouldn't let me get a new drill; I could have put my finger on it straight away."

"But did you notice he took much longer to find the item required than the store man at No 1 factory?"

"There was a lot more in his stores than in the smaller stores. Can't you understand that?"

Douglas leaned forward almost touching noses, "I understand that, but do you?"

Cledwyn sat back, "Of course I do, but what's the moral to the story?"

Douglas stood up, "No 2 had a bigger capacity up at his stores; a little more time was needed to search." Douglas peered down at the paper in Cledwyn's hand, "You've smudged the writing on your paper," he said. "Just like the store man at No 1 you haven't the capacity in your store when you take in a new delivery."

Cledwyn's eyes widened with madness and he sat there staring, angry and speechless.

The train, on its return journey, sounded its whistle and came chugging into the halt. It stopped to leave the passengers off for refreshments and to admire the scenery. Douglas stood and walked off, not even saying goodbye.

Cledwyn sat there for some moments, his eyes stabbing his mate in the back as Douglas disappeared down the lane. Then he smiled; my mate couldn't have meant what he said, he thought. But later, when he drove after him and stopped to give him the usual lift home, Douglas had cold eyes and deliberate words.

"I want nothing off you," he said, softly. "You won't see me next week; you have inspired in me a desire to seek a new vocation."

"Have I really? That's wonderful."

"From now on I am going to be..." he glanced at Cledwyn. "A Loner." And he walked off.

Cledwyn put his foot down on the accelerator and sped away, not understanding his mate at all.

Flame of the Candle

Life's like a flame of a candle.
Sometimes it stands erect and bright,
Sometimes it flickers agitating the night.
Caught unawares by an opening door
It becomes overburdened,
Gives light no more.
But the smoke and aroma
That comes from the flame
Ascends to the heavens and suffers no pain.

The Maverick

The brass ferrule of his walking stick clicked on the footpath as he walked stiffly, dark glasses hiding his scarred eyes. Thin red skin from the acid burn stretched down his left cheek. He could hear the leaves moving in the oak trees, and detected empty crisp packets surfing along the road. He couldn't remember noticing such soft sounds before.

"We'll sit here on this bench," said Gina, his wife. "My legs are tired."

He recognised the place where they sat, the smell of lavender from the perfumed shrubbery gave it away. The park was familiar to him blind as when he had sight.

"Can you smell the lavender?" asked Gina.

"There's nothing wrong with my nose."

His arm was straight, resting on his vertical cane, his body rigid. Gina had waited a year to see him smile again, but each day was a disappointment.

"There's a child laughing," said Malcolm, tersely, as though he disapproved.

Gina new it was his way of wanting to know more. "It's a little boy with an old man, grandfather I suppose. They're going down the steps towards the lake, there are lots of people sitting around the lake today."

"Any kids on the swings?"

"Yes. And there's a few splashing around in the pool."

Gina didn't volunteer too much imagery, she had to be diplomatic since his attack. It was difficult to know what to say without him snapping or misinterpreting her words. He had refused to face the world, gave up on people and blamed God for his misfortune. After months of failed gentle persuasion she'd decided to be sharp with him; it worked. Today he had agreed to accompany her for the first time since that terrible night a year ago when they'd rushed him to hospital screaming, the paramedics had held his arms to stop him scraping the flesh from his face. Later, when he'd calmed down and the painkillers relieved his suffering, he'd coolly said, "Those druggies have ended my life." He'd tried to reason with them, but their arms had hung loosely, eyes vacant and staring, too *high* to take in his logic. Calling the police was the only answer.

"Are you bored with me?" he blurted. "Nothing to say?"

"I've already given you the usual details, love." She touched her head against his. "Your standing orders."

"The people staring at us Don't know, at least pretend we're talking."

"There is nobody staring. I've got my white sleeveless blouse on and a navy-blue fitted skirt. Two inches below the knee, as requested."

"Your hair?"

"Permed and curled around my ears."

He briefly pictured her soft oval face framed by her ebony curled hair, and then imagined his own grotesque image. He shuddered. "Good. Stay young." What he wanted to say was, stay with me.

She felt the vibes of his insecurity, shouldered him playfully. "I can't work miracles, Malcolm."

"Last night I dreamt I had my eyesight back. Then I woke up."

She clasped his hand. "That would be a miracle, love."

There's a twist in it. In the dream I had grown old and ugly."

"That's awful! Let's change the subject."

She hadn't told him his hair had begun to turn white a month after the attack, within six months there wasn't a black hair left in his head. He was the same age as her, forty, but now he looked ten years older; his face thinner and scarred. If they could have had children maybe life would have taken a different turn. Maybe it's my fault for being barren, she thought. His youth club and church seemed to have taken the place of paternal expectations.

"You've gone quiet again," he said.

"Do you want an ice cream?"

"It'll be something to do."

"Do you want to come with me, or stay here?"

"I'm enough of a spectacle here, I Don't want to be waiting in that claustrophobic shed they call a cafe. Don't be long."

He listened to the clicking of her shoes diminishing. He pictured her walking up the road to the shop/cafe. She's passing the toilets, the colourful shrubbery, then the sound died and he suddenly felt the loneliest of men. The warm breeze carried the laughter of the children playing in the distant recreation area. He heard a dog bark, a big dog, he knew that, at a guess a Labrador. Black or sandy? Huh! He'd have to rely on charity for that answer. Then the distinctive voice of a child coming closer."

"Oh, no, no, no," it said. He didn't like the sound, yet it wasn't a fearful protest, a little boy, he thought. Then a man's voice, "Oh, yes, yes, yes," laughed the man. It was a deep pretentious voice. They kept repeating. Then all went quiet. The little boy's voice again. "Man over there Bampa—funny glasses." His grandfather looked at Malcolm and whispered. "Shush. I think He's blind."

"Sorry," said the grandfather as he approached. "He's only three and half, the age of innocence."

Malcolm said, abruptly, "What's all that yes, yes, yes, and no, no, no, about?"

"It's a little tease. Like the bulldog advert on the TV add."

The child took in a sharp breath and pointed. "Man face, Bampa."

"Quiet, Dafydd. Come on, I'd better take you for your lolly. Sorry once again."

"Innocent children Don't bother me."

The grandfather looked at the bitter, scarred face of Malcolm. He felt a mixture of sympathy and curiosity intriguing him. He sat beside him, still holding the boy's hand.

"I'm sorry, it must have been a terrible accident."

Malcolm tightened his grip on his stick. "It was no accident! I've been turned into a bizarre attraction by mindless thugs."

"Attacked? Good grief!"

He clenched his teeth. "Druggies! Nutters."

"There are times when life doesn't make sense, does it? Atrocities all over the world, innocent people suffering, probably some answer to it all, somewhere."

A bloody philosopher thought Malcolm. That's all I need.

The attack and the pain of sizzling flesh suddenly came back: His eyes inflating to the point of explosion, his lids like vices trying to shut out the burning pain. He suddenly burst with emotion. "They had a good damned reason! I wouldn't let them in the youth club. I called the police but they ran off. They came back later masked. Threw acid in my face and took the club's money. Laughing! That's a damn good reason!"

The old man realised he had upset Malcolm, yet he wanted to help calm the anger and sorrow he felt coming from him. "I understand," he said almost in a whisper. "It must have been hell!".

"Come on, Bampa, I want a Lolly."

"Say please, Dafydd."

"Pees, Bampa."

"Take him," said Malcolm," thinking he'd frightened the child.

The little boy pointed at Malcolm's hair. "God's hair, Bampa?"

"Yes, the same as Bampa's."

Malcolm stiffened. "What's he talking about?" he said.

"My hair's white. I tell him it's the same colour as God's."

Malcolm brushed his hair with his hand feeling the same familiar softness. "Is my hair white? Ha! God's done a good job!"

The old man shook his head. "It's strange how people sometimes blame God for the tragedies of the world."

"The devil looks after his own."

"Friend, I wouldn't wish your trouble on my worst enemy, but it's not fair for Dafydd to be given the wrong impression of the Almighty. Perhaps we'd better leave you."

"That's right. Walk away. Question God and away they go." But the old man detected a plaintive tone in Malcolm.

"I can see you are coping with your accident most admirably my friend, but Don't let Satan kill your spirit."

"Talk is cheap."

"I once knew a lady who became blind in late life, caused by glaucoma. "I'm glad I'm not deaf," she told me. "I can see all my memories within, but if I were deaf and saw Pavarotti singing, he'd look silly with no sound."

"I've got memories; helping children, collecting for charity, raising funds for the church. Where did it get me?"

"Church?" questioned the old man. "Too much pomp and ceremony for me," he said, his voice trailing off into a soliloquy. "I'm a man of silent meditation; all that hymn singing, medieval chanting and repetitive prayers; gaudy robes and stain-glass windows. Why, that's nothing to do with God. Those additions only please vain aspirations. Man cannot better the creations of God."

Malcolm tapped his stick impatiently. "Where's that wife of mine?"

"Come on, Bampa. Let's go."

The grandfather pulled a bag of sweets from his pocket and gave it to the little boy. Dafydd accepted and stared at Malcolm.

"Won't be long, Dafydd. Then he turned back to Malcolm. "Reverse your philosophy. You'll be a lot happier if you do."

Malcolm never thought a great deal of his personal philosophy. "Philosophy!" he snapped. "I haven't got a philosophical thought in my head. I'm a practical man."

"Your philosophy is that God is responsible for everything that happens. That makes him all-powerful. Therefore, if He is that great, surely He can rid this world of the Satan. No, my belief is that the Devil and God have equal powers. If it were not so, one would have eliminated the other by now. Mankind is at the centre of the cosmic scales, and whichever way mankind moves, he gives the balance of power to that force."

Malcolm began to wish he hadn't accused the old man of walking away. Now he could feel his hot breath on his burnt cheek and the warm hand of Dafydd on his knee. He sensed the boy looking at him and wondered why he hadn't recoiled in horror.

"It's a convenient theory," he said with a sceptical tone."

"It keeps *me* going," the old man emphasised, wasting a kindly smile on the blind man. "When you follow the path of God you must tread carefully. For if you give Him weight, the Devil loses strength. God is a God of Love and incapable of hurting his creation. Therefore, what happened to you was the work of the Devil."

"Bampa, man no?."

"Man can't see, Dafydd."

"What's the boy saying?"

"He's offering you a sweet. Marshmallow."

"No thank you, boy."

"Oh Yes, yes, yes," Dafydd said.

"You've started him off now. You'll have to accept or say, no, no, no, no, in a deep voice."

Malcolm held out his hand and Dafydd placed a sticky sweet in it.

"Bampa, go now?"

"Come on then. Let's get you a lolly. Say bye to the man."

"Bye man."

Malcolm reluctantly nodded his head. It was his first step back into the caring world. He couldn't let the boy go believing he was bitter against such innocence. Both the boy and the old man had treated him as normal. With a quiet voice he said, "Bye Dafydd. Thank you for the sweet."

The old man tapped Malcolm gently on his knee. "You must have been very close to God for the devil to have singled you out," he said. "Have faith, for your sight is to be restored in the right place at the chosen time. Maybe not in this life, but you'll see again."

Malcolm sighed submissively. "You'd make a good rector."

The old man chuckled softly. "The sermon of a rector is shackled by the doctrine of his sect. He has to hold his tongue in case he offends his superiors or breaks the ecclesiastical rules. A lot of them are hypocrites, you know. But I'd rather see a world full of churchgoers than a street full of the ungodly. At times, however, even a bishop needs to show his own true feelings. Goodbye, friend. And, thank you."

Gina came back a few moments later sounding impatient. "One person serving; The poor girl was red in the face catering for teas, sandwiches and ice-cream." She handed Malcolm his cone. "What did the clergyman have to say?"

"Clergyman?"

"The old man with the child, he was wearing a clerical collar and red breast piece."

A flicker of a smile came to Malcolm's face and he gave the situation some thought. "He's what I'd call a clerical maverick."

Gina appeared puzzled, but didn`t comment. "Did you talk much?"

"Enough, I suppose."

They sat licking their ice-creams, saying very little to each other until they finished.

"Are you ready to go back, love?" she asked him.

"Gina, you've been trying to get me back down the youth club this past couple of months. Do you think I'll be of any use?"
She had to control herself, for she felt her emotions begin to overflow. Quite firmly she said, "They *need* you down there, Malcolm. You organise things so well, you have a duty to go there."

"Right," he said quietly, "Perhaps I should make a start next Wednesday. Now that I've made the decision, I shall look forward to it."

They stood up and a great heaviness lifted from Gina. It wasn't so much the decision he had made that overwhelmed her, it was the softness that had come back in his voice.

The Microscopic Soul

Squeezed from a pore
Of human skin,
He hovered above a mountain range
Of fleshy slopes
And craggy bones.
Ecstatic at the revelation,
Released from the body's incarceration,
He was to be taken home.

He stretched his delicate transparent arms
And felt his crown of silver curls,
Caressed his lower golden fleece,
Touched his face of polished pearl.
All sense of blood and nerves had gone,
Shed in that temporal case.
Caught suddenly in magnetic breeze
He was drawn at speed to outer space.

No sense of time or travel,
Though yellow beads of stars shot past.
Neither heat nor cold could penetrate
The protective shield of God's caress
He left the galaxies behind
Without cosmic sensation,
Impatient to be reconciled
With the Lord of all creation.

In the distance, an amber orb,
Flood-lit by a ring of suns:
A gigantic sphere in perpetual light,
Suspended in warmth where life began.
He cruised across spiritual lands,

Reflecting in orange lakes,
Across plumaged woods and floral hills,
Sweet music followed his breezy wake.
Ahead a shining mist appeared:
A mass of guardian souls.
They took him to the holy spot,
And joined more joyful crowds.
A paternal voice pervaded:
A welcome to the holy shrine.
He was safe, complete, contented.
All evil he'd known was left behind.

Davey's Mission

God created the four Elements to bring harmony to the universe," said Sheenagh, galaxy Controller of Water, as she paced the marble floor. "Implanting seeds of destiny is the only answer," she continued as she held her sharp features aloft, white hair hanging down her back, sleeveless, turquoise robe covering her slender body. "Element Earth is easily led. Fire is devious! Water is the only cosmic power acting responsibly."

"Element Air is no better. It has fickle ways!" agreed Lovegood, second in command. "Our method is extreme but it prevents the most gifted of figure-heads succumbing to the temptations of Fire. We are merely doing what Fire has done to other planets. It is our duty to redress the balance of good and evil."

"Hetarra must be next," said Sheenagh, inspecting her long, blue fingernails. But first we must eliminate the evil Fire. "Fire must not dominate!"

"Expediency is essential," Lovegood warned.

Sheenagh slumped in her throne-like seat, her arms outstretched on the cushioned armrests, her blue lips contrasting the snowy whiteness of her face. Her turquoise eyes turned to the open glass doors of the control room. Beyond the pillared terrace the extensive garden brought sweet fragrances. She wanted to rest and enjoy the sounds of the distant rivulets splashing. In her mind's eye she could see the creaminess of the full moon sparkling on the gentle rippling waters. A faint smile came to her face remembering the times she sat in solitude on the bank of her favourite river.

Lovegood went to the window, sweeping his white robe behind his frail body.

"Where are we to start?" he said, softly. "We have not visited Hetarra for two thousand years."

"Complacent Element Earth should have maintained our standards. Flora, fauna and aquatic life suffer whilst Earth stoops to Fire. Give me an update on Hetarra."

Lovegood pressed a series of buttons on the nearby console, and then brushed his shock of springy white hair with bony fingers. A screen lit up on the white marble wall and began to run through the millenniums. The twentieth century flashed as being the most destructive era in Hetarra`s existence. Lovegood read the information:

"The people of Hetarra have been influenced by Fire's interpretation of progress, introducing 92 minor elements, causing sloth and complacency and naivety, creating aggression and leaving the population confused. The principle of the sacred Four Elements has been driven from the minds of civilisation giving power to few and misery to many."

"That is typical of Fire. The peoples of the galaxy are victims. The Elements were for enjoyment, but Fire made them gods. Ask lieutenant Davey to come here."

Davey, a young Iceman hooked on adventure, arrived. He wore only a long white sleeveless robe, revealing a bare chest. His transparent azure body displayed a powerful rolling mist within, though his sharp features expressed amusement. Smiling insincerely, he bowed in an automatic manner.

"My lady has an assignment for me?" A cold vapour emitted from his lips.

"Something that will keep you occupied for decades if not centuries. I want you to go to Hetarra. We need to recapture the minds of principals, but first we need to locate the galaxy control centre of Fire."

Davey placed his hands on his blue spiked hair and swung round to Lovegood, "Another reconnaissance mission?"

Lovegood smiled. "This time, your task will be passive. You know the drill. Lie dormant in the mind of a native and send back information through its senses. Fire is very active on Hetarra, but its control headquarters is not there. We must locate it. We will be orbiting and picking up data from you."

Davey was disappointed. "It's not the galaxy-busting mission I expected."

"We will influence your surrogate mother to name you Davey," Sheenagh said.

"Find the control centre of Element Fire," said Lovegood. "We believe it's somewhere in Hetarra's galaxy. That's your mission!"

"On Hetarra?"

"Hetarra will be central and appropriate."

"What procedures do I undergo?"

"You will be miniaturised and transplanted into a Hettarean foetus. You will enter the world of Hetarra as all humans do.

* * *

Davey's mother had seen her three older children off to school and began the laundry wash. Rubbing on the washing board in the oblong stone sink, the block of green soap wore away. She looked under the sink between the brick-built supports. "Damn!"

Rolling down the sleeves of her navy cardigan she took her coat from behind the door. "You stay on that settee," she said to three-year-old Davey, still in his cream flannelette night-shirt. "Mam's going across the road to the market." Davey looked at her, his warm body lethargic after another night of bad dreams. Last night the air-raid siren had wailed, frightening him and making his body shiver from fright.

"Don't be long," he pleaded as she opened the door.

The sound of people walking through the slushy February morning, chatting and complaining, came through the door, and then it closed and went quiet again. The coal fire radiated between two black-lead ovens relaxing him, his body weary, his mind lacking interest in play. He is fascinated by the yellow and amber flames winding their way through the coals, dancing like genies until they turn to smoke and get sucked up the chimney. The fire brightens. Faces appear and stare back at him with piercing blood-filled eyes. Red hot bodies emerge from the flames, slip on to the hearth and grow long, burning limbs. The shimmering naked Fire People, male and female, weaving and jinking, sidle towards him spreading pungent sulphur. They slide up on to the settee. Davey expects the sofa to ignite, but his surroundings darken and fade into another time zone.

A strident voice: "Atomise him."

Their eyes shoot yellow rays causing a humming throughout his body, disintegrating him to a silver dust cloud. And then nothing, no pain, no trauma, no sound. Suddenly he is above the wintry atmosphere and the Fire People have disappeared. He hurtles through space seeing planets and asteroids shoot past as though he is a single eye, his atomised body following like a comet's tail.

On and on he travels until there is nothing but blackness. Then a vague light ahead begins to grow to brilliance. He perceives a colourful planet with several suns giving permanent light. He descends rapidly, precipitated into its orbital path: a continent, a country, a building and then, darkness.

He hears the same piercing voice. "Materialise!"

Regaining his form he finds himself kneeling, spotlighted on a round smouldering platform, glowing in a large room of subdued light. An intense heat pervades, yet he feels no great pain, though his tongue is swollen and dry and his nose stings from acrid sheaths of coral smoke undulating around him. He tries to murmur but his voice does not respond. It's not like the other nightmares, he is awake but powerless and being controlled. An inner force manipulate his eyes and pan the area straining to capture the scene, focusing on the blistering Fire People who stand around on guard, burning with a quivering spectrum. The voice again:

"Awaiting examination."

The vast hall illuminates showing a series of suspended platforms at varied levels and different colours, like large surfboards glowing with phosphorescence.

A door opens at the far end of the hall; a burst of orange light, in the midst a silhouette of a figure sitting on a moving disc making quickly towards Davey. It is a man sitting cross-legged, wearing a black cloak. Only his red leathery face and bald veined head can be seen. It's a severe, sharp face with high cheek bones and long pointed chin. He comes to rest near Davey. A sinewy hand snakes from under the gown and slowly moves up to his dry wizened countenance. The limb scratches its long crimson nose then slides back under the gown. His cracked lips part and a shrill voice utters from a black hole.

"This one is too old for predestine!"

The strident voice: "He volunteered."

"Planet? Millennium? Century? Decade?"

"Hetarra. Millennium number two, nineteen hundred and forty three."

"We are in command of that era! Have we not got them murdering and bombing each other with their primitive weapons? Disciples are not required! Fool!"

"He called us through our element."

"He is clearly not Fire. Look how he suffers. You have been tricked!"

"It was apparent..."

"Apparent! Apparent! Get out you fool. Your second-in-command will take instructions!"

In his place stepped a shimmering female and bowed reverently.

"Take the Hettarean to the laboratory and scan his every cell for an alien force." He drew the loose hood around his face, the disc he sat on turned, moved sharply and disappeared through the aperture from which it came. Davey`s platform was drawn through a sliding door of blinding light, followed by the new female commander of the guards.

* * *

"They're on to us, commander, warned Lovegood," viewing Davey's progress on the screen.

"Davey has done his job well. So their headquarters is on the planet of Scramasia. Is the task force in position?"

"There are three thousand Icemen in the stratosphere, battle stations and dart shuttles on alert just waiting for confirmation of the planet they are to destroy."

"Scramasia! Attack, and then flood the planet when all are eliminated. The affluent natives have predestined seeds of Fire within them. They have no morals. Cruelty is their entertainment. Scramasia is a hopeless case, it must die. The poor are contaminated with ignorance. Water will destroy in seven days what 92 minor elements have taken centuries to build. Pure life must rebirth elsewhere."

"It shall be done, Commander. What of Davey?"

"Return him to his time zone on Hetarra. Davey will be the first seed of predestination to save that world. He can go down from generation to generation. We will find him a partner when we are ready to colonise an earlier time zone."

Before the Fire people had chance to operate on Davey, the doors of the theatre exploded open. Icemen burst in, their transparent bodies revealing the glowing blue inner power generated for battle. Beams of indigo light hissed from their mouths rendering the Fire People to black corpses, disintegrating them to clouds of vapour. Some fought back with eyeball lasers, squelching Icemen to fluids sizzling on the floor. The fight continued throughout the complex, making every room a battle zone, disintegrating controls and exploding communications.

The Fire General instigated his contingency plans and fled to the roof of the burning building to his escape craft. Sheenagh had anticipated such a move and was ready for him. The golden, diamond-shaped, vessel was blown back to the surface of the planet bursting into a fireball. Soon the Icemen reported the complete destruction of Fire's command post, leaving the headquarters a burning mountain. Sheenagh instructed them to return. The sky quickly filled with silver dart-shaped crafts to pick them up. Icemen boarded and then disappeared into the stars as quickly as they had come.

Soon, heavy clouds crept over the continents of Scramasia slowly hiding the light, blanking out the suns until there was nothing but blackness. People from cities and villages, who were taught life was endless under the Fire People, emerged from houses and leisure domes panicking and screaming as generators stopped. Blinding flashes of lightening suddenly lit up the land, followed by an ear-blasting explosion of thunder. Another and then another. Huge globules of rain crashed down on everything causing a rapid build-up of high water. Escarpments that had been stable for centuries crumbled, creating rivers of raging debris, burying buildings, humans and animals. Meadows turned to lakes, valleys flooded, mountains submerged drowning the hot blood of a selfish planet. As quickly as it started it ended. Clouds parted and the sun broke through. Where once stood a prosperous and evil regime, now spread a clear blue ocean from horizon to horizon. In the distance, could be seen a lone sailing vessel searching for high ground.

Davey screamed to consciousness on the settee and looked for his mother.

"Nasty dream again, love? I wish you'd tell me about the nightmares you have."

Davey held his arms to her. She picked him up and nursed him.

Joe

Contented now with balanced brain,
The accident has made his name.
Those days have gone when he stole the roads
With uncombed hair and Burberry coat,
Scuffed boots tied with half a lace,
Worn and grey as his bitter face.
His confidence had turned to shame,
His search for work was endless pain,
His social life so far astray
He would not pass the time of day.

He crossed the road, could not say where,
His mind was blank and void of care,
He wakened in a hospital bed,
Despair had been knocked from his head.
There was peace and warmth and love at last,
No haunting memories of the past.
No sorrow from his lack of gifts,
No longing to be idly rich,
No envy of exalted birth,
No contempt for pretentious mirth.

Now with his invalidity
He lifts his glass for all to see.
His facial grin is full of bliss
He sips his pint and gives a kiss.
His happiness pervades the room,
He thinks He's won the football pools.
Immune, oblivious, he shouts hello!
And everyone responds to Joe.
Was it Satan's hand or Lady Luck,
Or God's grace saying, Joe's had enough?

Dewi Diago

The concert hall of the Cwm Morlais Rugby Club was already smoky, and the noise from the customers, loud and cheerful. Dewi Diago, in his sixties, and Ron who was in his middle fifties, stood at the bar sipping their beers, waiting to begin the entertainment. Dewi, a good six inches taller than Ron's five feet six, was in a thoughtful mood which didn't go unnoticed by his friend.

"You alright, Dewi?" asked Ron.

"I could have done with a bit more notice," he replied, in his baritone voice.

"You're an old trouper, don't worry."

"What charity is it for, anyway?"

"I don't know."

"There's a lot of familiar faces here tonight," remarked Dewi.

"All credit to the artists turning up for charity," enthused Ron

"You're going to play for me, aren't you Ron?"

"I always do, don't I?"

"I'll need you backing towards the end of the night. I'll sing Diana first, and then Ten Guitars to finish off."

Ron looked around at the sheaths of cigarette smoke thickening the atmosphere, aided and abetted by the aroma of his cigar and Dewi's cigarette.

"They're beginning to get noisy, Dewi. I see the steward is making his way to the stage, I think you're on. Get them before they get too boisterous."

Dewi took a last gulp of his pint then asked the girl behind the bar for another, noticing she only gave half a smile. "You alright, Sheila?"

"Yea I'm fine Dewi," she said, avoiding his eyes.

"Sheila's quiet tonight," he said to Ron. "She's normally quite chatty."

"It's a busy night for her," replied Ron.

They looked to the stage as the steward demanded order and called

Dewi Diago up to compere the evening's proceedings as he always did. An ironic cheer erupted from the capacity crowd as Dewi made his way through the congestion carrying his pint, careful not to knock the drink-filled tables. He took the microphone off the steward and stood there with a big smile on his round, ruddy face, his full head of black hair neatly combed. He paused until the room fell quiet then prepared himself to narrate his latest joke. True, it would be Dewi's latest joke, but the crowd waited in anticipation to see if it would be a new one or an old tried and tested one. His tall, full figure, still showing the muscular potential that had been beneficial to him as a collier, was impressive and commanded attention. Tonight, his patter was a list of the many local artists who were going to be called up to give a song when the guest trio had done its act. And so, Dewi began his introductions: "Now I want the best of order tonight because we have artists from all over the country." Ironic laughter. "For example we have Billy Evans, just finished a season in Blackpool, Phil Bevan who is in pantomime in London, specially down for the show. Danny Diamond, just arrived from Las Vegas after being supporting artist to Tom Jones, and many more who have come from around Britain to give their talents for this worthy charity we are all supporting."

The audience encouraged him with laughter and applause knowing the artists are all known locals.

A spectacled, middle-aged man standing at the bar, a stranger to the club, and a little intoxicated after his rugby team had lost to Cwm Morlais, was perplexed and moody at having his intelligence put to question. He sidled up to Ron and was surprised to find him smiling and apparently enjoying the entertainment.

"You don't believe that rubbish do you?" he said to Ron.

Ron, seeing the gullibility of his neighbour, thought he would play along with him for a time. "You can bet your bottom dollar," he said in an American accent. "Dewi Diago knows all the top acts."

The stranger turned to his pint. "Rubbish! If they're that good what the hell are they doing in a rugby club?"

Ron dropped his American accent and turned to the stranger. "You're serious aren't you? Of course it's nonsense. It's a bit of fun."

"And that mop of black hair?" queried the man. "He's not got a grey hair in it."

"Dewi's toupee; it comes off for the summer."

The man's face reddened with embarrassment for being taken in so easily. "And the name, why do they call him Dewi Diago, anyway?" he asked humbly. "That's an odd mixture of cultures."

"Oh, now that's serious. I can tell you that story. Something Dewi is very proud of."

The stranger, realising he was in company with a friend of the compere, thought he'd better show more respect.

"It sounds very interesting. I'd like to hear it."

"Dewi likes to have a bit of order for the first five minutes, at least, Just like all us artists, so give him a chance."

"Sorry. I just wanted to show a bit of interest. I've never heard anyone called Dewi Diago before."

Dewi continued. "Last week the teacher asked my grandson why did they bury Henry VIII in Westminster Abbey? Now my grandson is very good at history and he was puzzled for a while, but then it came to him. I know, Miss, he said. Because he was dead."

The audience laughed and cheered to Diago's jokes as he created a friendly and jovial atmosphere. Some chuckled and sipped their drinks as Dewi warmed them up in readiness for the first artist.

"Well, come on," said the stranger at the bar. "Let's hear the story."

Ron looked at him with a suspicious eye. "Are you sure?"

"Of course I'm sure, I wouldn't say it if I wasn't."

"Have you ever been down a pit or drift?"

"No. I'm an office worker."

"You wouldn't appreciate it."

"Try me, man. Try me!"

Ron looked up to the stage, which was twenty yards away from him, and saw his mate in full flow, now oblivious to anyone who was not fully attentive:

"And that's not all, ladies and gentlemen. In the audience tonight we have folk from Brecon Rise, where the money-people come from, and from Dallas. No, not Dallas Texas, but from Dallas Top, just down the road.

Ron smiled at the familiar stories, and then turned to the stranger. "Where you from?"

"Cwmllynflell."

"Cwm what?"

"I can only say it once. I haven't been living there long. Cwm...lly...We played you today."

"Oh. That's the team we beat today."

"Don't remind me. I've left them in the other room... bus comes at midnight."

"Forget about it. Enjoy yourself. You'll appreciate the artists, I'm sure."

"You were going to tell me about Dewi."

"Alright, but Dewi has done a bit of boxing in his time, so I wouldn't be cynical about it. It was in 1962 in the Trelewis drift mine. Dewi was on the dayshift and we were making our way down the two-mile-long five-foot tunnel to the coal face along with twenty others."

"You were there?"

"Oh aye, I was there. Me and Dewi walked behind the rumbling spake, a carriage with unglazed windows which took the boys to the face. Our helmet lamps cast golden beams as we squelched through the darkness, the water seeped through the roof and dripped on our helmets and made black murky pools at our feet, and the smell of coal dust came up from the face...."

"Oh god," mumbled the stranger. "What have I done? Not another collier spitting out lumps of coal."

"What?"

"Nothing, carry on."

"Anyway, as we neared the face and the roof became lower, the spake came to a halt and we heard a distinctive creaking which stopped the whole shift in our tracks. We listened intently hardly daring to breath, but all we could hear was the echoing sound of water dripping into puddles..." Ron paused and gave Dewi a quick, respectful hearing.

"Now in the first half we will have these young up-and-coming rockers who's amplifiers and speakers fill the stage - no room to move here, mun. In the second half we will call up the first five artists, and in the third half we will have the other five artists. Stop tap is early tonight two am. But the committee told me if you behave yourselves we'll have a fourth half which will take us on a little longer...."

The stranger, wishing to win some kind of point, nudged Ron. "He's not quite right there," he said. "You can't have a third half. There are only two halves. If you split it in three it becomes thirds."

"What's your name, anyway?" asked Ron.

"Jack. Jack Evans."

For the first time Ron studied the stranger. His five-foot five, stout figure was smartly dressed: A navy blazer, white shirt with a fine red stripe and a pale red tie to match. His grey hair was wavy and kept in place by shining cream. His fine intelligent-looking face didn't match his wit, thought Ron.

"Well, Jack Evans, Dewi Diago can have has many halves as he likes, unless you want to put him right on the subject of fractions and grammar?"

"No, no. What happened down the drift mine, you were saying?"

"Where was I. Oh... So we were worried about this creaking, because the only things that creak down there are the timbers holding the roof up. The men got out of the spake and stood in silence. Another loud creak. We all looked in the same direction simultaneously, and there it was: a cracked roof beam near the coal face which could come down any minute. Now, in that area we had what we called "walking chocks", metal cubed frameworks which had six legs, two handles in front and two in the rear. It was constructed of boxed steel and weighed two hundredweight. They were for placing under the roof beams to support them in such a dangerous situation as we had. These walking chocks are normally lifted by two men, one in the front and one in rear. Dewi could see the immediate danger. He raced for a chock, got inside it, grabbed at the side bars and heaved. His muscles bulged like oranges. "Heave", he yelled, as the chock lifted, and he waddled across the sludge and wedged it under the cracking beam just as it was slowly coming down. Seconds later we would have been buried under a load of rock and rubble."

Ron was interrupted when a loud applause accompanied Dewi from the stage. The compere had introduced the rock band and was making his way to the bar, chatting to a number of people as he came. Ron, seeing Dewi's hands where empty having left his pint somewhere, ordered another lager for him and his mate took a few grateful gulps as soon as he got to the bar. Then the rock trio burst into sound and conversation became difficult. However, Dewi raised his strong voice above the loud music to air his apprehension to Ron.

"I'm not happy, Ron," he shouted.

"What's up?"

"I've been trying to find out about this charity we're supporting, but nothing is coming up."

I expect it's all above board, Dewi, said Ron."

"There's no talk of where the money is, who it's for. Nothing. Now you know me, Ron. I've got a good name to protect. I don't ask anything for my troubles and I don't want anything. I've promoted and organised charities for years and I've always been told who's collecting and what it's in aid of."

"I'm sure it will be alright, Dewi."

"No! I'm not having it, I'm going to finish this pint now and sort it out with the organisers."

"You've got a busy night as compere, Dewi. Leave it to me. I know who's organising it. I'll go and ask a few questions to put your mind at rest."

"Would you do that for me, Ron? I'd be very grateful."

"You concentrate on the festivities. I'll do a little digging."

Ron left, giving the barmaid a knowing wink and taking his drink with him, leaving Dewi at the crowded bar, and the stranger, Jack Evans, looking up at him.

"Excuse me, Mr Diago," he said. Your friend was telling me how you came to be called Dewi Diago."

Dewi grinned at the man. "He told you that, did he?"

"He didn't quite finish, actually. He got as far as you wedging a walking chock under a beam, but it didn't equate with the name Dewi Diago."

Dewi's eyes squinted at the stranger. "I was the only one who could lift a walking chock on my own. But in in Italy at that time there was a strongman who was famous for his strength— "Dynamic Diago" he was known as. Well, when the boys saw me carrying that chock on my own, somebody said, "Look at Dewi, he's like Dynamic Diago of Italy." So they called me Dewi Diago, and the name has stuck ever since."

The stranger nodded, looking disappointed, thinking that the reason might have been more interesting.

There was a rush to the bar and Dewi moved away to a table where some of the artists sat. It was convenient from there to reach the stage and introduce them. As the evening progressed and the smell of cigars thickened and the crowd sang along with the guitars, Ron appeared and gave Dewi the thumbs up, easing his apprehension. Too noisy to be heard, Ron motioned he'd explain later.

At 11 O'clock, one of the organisers of the charity decided to take to the stage, surprising Dewi, as he wasn't used to being usurped by an organiser. However, he was glad of the break and sat down. After calling for order and the crowd became quiet, the organiser spoke.

"Good evening all. What a wonderful night we are having and, I assure you, it is to continue. But first I have a little announcement to make on behalf of us all. The majority of you know the reason why we are here tonight. It's not to collect for charity, but to show our appreciation to one of our big-hearted characters. If we had told him our plans he might not have turned up, but saying it is for charity, he came willingly.

Over the years, he has helped to organise many charities and has gained thousands of pounds for worthy causes. He tried to play down the fact that he is 65 years of age to day and didn't want any fuss. But we couldn't let the day pass without showing our gratitude to the man who has done so much over the years. He asks for no thanks, but you have all come tonight for one reason, and that is to wish Dewi Diago the happiest of birthdays. Happy birthday, Dewi Diago."

There was a terrific roar from the crowd as they all stood up and sang the birthday melody to Dewi. But more was to come, for as the ditty was being sung, ten artists with ten guitars gathered around the stage. Then Dewi was called up and given the microphone. He knew what he had to sing. With choked throat and glassy eyes, he sang his favourite song, Ten Guitars.

The Old Man at the River

Sleeping below the parapet wall
Outside the Bridgend Inn,
Where blackberry tendrils, like
Gorgon's hair,
Give up sweet fruit for all to share,
He lazed along with the river Usk
Amid Crickhowell's contented scene.
Slow water rolled over the weir
Falling into the blue of the sky.
His body rested in the earth,
As in his mother
Before the birth.
Concentric ripples yawned,
The river became alive.

Fish belly-flopped on top of the dam
Spinning rainbow cascades,
Full of seeds for the spawning ground,
No time to stop or swim around,
They danced away from the pull
Of the edge,
Disappearing to darker shades.

There he sat, his spawning done,
Life's cycle ending.
The stepping stones from
Life to death
Have taken him to his last breaths.
No seeds to give, no strength to swim,
He is, it seems, awaiting Heaven.

Drifting from the Fire

Drodon grunted in the darkness of the deep caves, his elongated features like an ant-eater's, his clothes ragged, his hairy body fine as a mole's pelt. Three generations of his family follow behind, groaning and wailing in discordant chorus. Anything would do, ants, worms, centipedes or, perhaps, some other flesh that was not of his family. He'll find the surface people one day, and then he'll have his revenge. He turned around, his deep gravelled voice admonishing:

"Stop your whimpering! You'd send a deaf rat scuttling."

His bedraggled wife pawed at her face, ensuring her long claws were turned away from her flat pink snout. She shuffled forward and caught up with him, brushing her long dishevelled hair over her arched back, "What's the use in going on? We might as well lie down and die. There's nothing left! Nothing!"

"They can't be underground. Must be near the surface. I've smelt the scented waste of luxury sieve through. We'll rise to the surface and have their soft pale flesh one day."

"Our tribe hasn't the strength to fight anymore."

"Hush, woman! I hear a faint drip of water. Quiet!" he yelled to everyone.

Shallow breathing could be heard as everyone strained their sensitive ears. The direction of the sound pin-pointed, they rushed to a high-roofed cave from where water dripped in many places. They lay on their backs scuffing around, long mouths agape, catching the droplets and sighing ecstatically. Drodon sampled and then followed the faint cold air that drifted from above, his long nose twitching excitedly.

"Stay here while I climb this slope," he growled.

The others took little notice, greedily gleaning the drops of unfrozen water seeping from the cracks in the roof of the cave. Such hostile conditions had driven their ancestors to the more hospitable caves, where they had lived on genetic tablet-food and subterranean streams until the water stopped flowing and their stockpile of tablets were exhausted. They had been promised such conditions wouldn't last forever; that a way would be found to compensate for the expanding galaxy, as the planet of Hetarra moved into the freezing zone of the solar system. Normality will return, they'd been promised long ago. It had happened to Stramasia and other planets, but Hetarra's scientists had promised their knowledge was greater and that they would find a solution to the planet's problems. It was a story handed down from generation to generation, century after century, before the continents dried up. The planet's natural resources had been exhausted and Hetarra became barren. The mountains and deserts froze over and food ran out. Water stopped flowing; Hetarra drifted further into darkness. It froze and died as it left the diminishing sun behind. The stench of cold decay had long gone, and the eerie echoing through the caverns of the howling prey had silenced. No longer do they have to smell their own family for recognition before an onslaught. Only Drodon and his family are left.

Drodon's wife instinctively moved to the far corner of the large cave and felt something soft on the rocks. It had the texture of moss, though she knew it couldn't be. She scraped some in her claws and pushed it into her mouth. It was insipid and damp on her tongue, yet nourishing. She scraped more and enjoyed it. The breaking of the subterranean fungus sent an odour to the others who raced to her. The sound of dull scratching echoed through the cave mixed with sighs and giggles, a musty smell rose from the scoured rocks.

Drodon had searched all his life for the elite surface people, as told in the legend. They betrayed his ancestors and still live in luxury within a self-sufficient dome near the surface. At times, he would climb to the open land above where he heard explosions and witnessed flashing in the night sky. The signs were too distant to follow on the perilous surface conditions, where life could freeze to death in an hour. But one day he'd find them. Then, all the humiliating, the digging with the bones of past victims, squeezing his brethren through small holes, scraping bellies under rocks to other tunnels, would be worth it.

* * *

In the southern quadrant beneath the floor of the valley, scientists were building a vessel that would take them to their salvation. In the massive underground workshop the huge catamaran-shaped spacecraft was about to be given its ultimate test. The high gantries and platforms had been removed giving it freedom to lift from the gigantic hole. Lights were losing their illumination as power-packs began to fade. Orders were given to board the catamaran. The Commander and the professor remained outside, watching the man-made base of the infertile valley slide open above them, revealing grey rocky slopes.

"This is it, Commander," said the professor, his ageing body bent and resting against the spacecraft.

"I know, prof," the stocky commander answered. "I reckon we needed more time."

"Our history has a lot to answer for. Wasted millenniums seeking power-thrones, believing man would last forever"

"Have we left it too late? Is this craft capable of reaching the planet of Sunevia?"

The professor hobbled to the entrance of the ship, stopped and turned. "Come on. We have nothing left except what's on board. It's now or never."

"We have fifty million miles to go. Can you imagine that?"

"Death is nearer. Our power units in this tomb won't last much longer."

"It's ironic we travel to a world in the solar system where our own planet once orbited."

"It has taken millions of years for Sunevia to take our place. Now we must reach it and recapture the warmth of the sun."

"We shouldn't be struggling to reach it, we should have been born there."

"Perhaps man evolves slower that the universe expands. Worldly power was always more important than space exploration. Come on before it's too late. We can planet-hop towards the sun but not away from it."

"As you say, it's too late to worry." The Commander half-heartedly saluted the massive cave then turned to enter the ship.

Suddenly, terrifying screams could be heard as a rumbling came from the far end of the huge workshop. The Commander climbed the ship's fixed ladder and stood on top of the spacecraft. He hardly believed his eyes. From a crevice in the rock at the far end of the underground came Drodon and his tribe. They screamed and ran manically towards the spaceship. The speed at which they were moving was unbelievable.

"God! Mutants!"

The Commander raced back down the ladder and pushed the professor inside. Activating the locking mechanism, he pulled his communication from his jacket pocket and ordered the Captain to close all entrances to the ship and energise the power reactors.

"Okay. Ignition now," said the Captain. "Is everything all right, Commander?"

"There are Mutants attacking the ship!"

The Control Captain remained cool as he and his assistants activated the controls. The massive roof of the underground workshop opened to its maximum and the atomic reactors created an explosion of fire beneath, lifting the craft through the choking cloud of fumes and dust. On the monitor screens, could be seen the grotesque figure of Drodon and his followers clambering desperately over the ship. They had scaled the outer ladders and were hammering their fists on the catamaran.

Inside the leisure room everybody was strapped in awaiting take-off. Two youngsters were looking through the porthole when one of the monsters came up against the glass. The teenage boy and girl screamed simultaneously attracting attention.

"What is it?" said the mother, and then screamed herself.

"Don't look," the father ordered. "We're safe in here."

Everybody strained at their straps watching the ugly savage trying to claw its way in.

"What is it father?" asked the girl.

"It's a mutant from the deep caves," answered an old man calmly. "I've seen one only once before. Forty years ago, I had to kill it or be killed."

The mutant opened its dog-like mouth in a scream then disappeared, as the catamaran lifted into the sky shedding the attackers one by one.

"They've gone," said the father. "Pitiful."

"Don't feel sorry for them," said the old man. "It was their ancestors who took our world to infertility by greed and stupidity."

The Commander raced to the control room central to the two great hulls. As he entered the Captain turned and gave him the thumbs up.

"Everything okay?"

"So far, Commander."

"Right. Everybody strap up. Captain, broadcast to all prefects to ensure all personnel are secured. Nobody is to unstrap until they are ordered."

Building to a speed of 11,500 miles per hour, the spacecraft broke the gravitation pull and soared into space. Fixed beneath each hull were two shuttles for emergency. A hundred pioneers made up of doctors, scientists, teachers, naturalists and their children were aboard the catamaran confident they would reach and inhabit their adopted planet of Sunevia.

Inter-linking corridors between the two hulls meant men women and children could travel freely by means of moving walkways. The only entertainment was to watch the complete history of their dying planet on virtual reality head-caps. They had everything on board to survive the arduous journey, except the knowledge that such an expedition had not been done before. Like the pioneers of the Old West, they only had their prayers and courage to keep them going.

With the planet's moon behind them, the journey progressed satisfactorily through silent star-glittering space. But as the weeks wore on problems arose when meteors glanced the spacecraft causing much damage. Simultaneously a deadly virus germinated and people began to die. Medics tried to identify the bacteria but time was not on their side, the virus struck with speed. As the disease spread through the craft, treatment rooms were quarantined where the hopeless cases were left to die. Their bodies became part of the cosmos as there was no alternative but to jettison them into space. Only fifty survived the first three weeks. More sections of the craft had to be shut down and made forbidden areas. Leisure rooms were contaminated and sealed off, food had been exposed to the virus and was ejected, water was rationed, medical supplies exhausted.

The Commander skilfully guided the wounded ship through outer space. The visual screen gave a panoramic view of the stars, though meteors passing at a safe distance reminded him of the vulnerability of the ship. The colourful glimmering sphere of Sunevia seemed to be within reach but the confidence of the ageing Commander was low. His robust build and determined chin would give an appearance of confidence, but his white, neglected hair, his lustreless blue eyes and sombre expression was an indication of the heaviness in his heart.

"At least we are still in path mode," said the Commander, as his Captain entered the control room. "How are the repairs progressing?"

"We're limping along. The rear of the right hull has been patched up but I can't take a chance on opening up the sealed rooms."

The Commander looked thoughtful. "The life of our world did not extend to inter-galaxy travel. It gave in too soon—what of the fatalities?"

"I had to eject another nine corpses, three more than yesterday... The prof will have to be buried in space as well."

The Commander turned in his control seat, shocked at the news. "The professor?"

The Captain sighed. "He went down fighting. Switch on the monitor on the rear power-pack room, Commander."

The Commander looked at his Captain with some anxiety, but switched the screen on. Prostrate on the floor lay the dead body of a young mutant, at its side, the professor."

"God! Where did it come from? What happened?"

"It must have got in when you and the prof were outside. I guess it was small enough to be the first to squeeze from the caves. It infested our ship. The professor must have realised this and went looking for it. He killed it, but not before the deadly virus took him.

The Commander thought for a second. "Are the families of Kantona and the Ranyon holding out?"

"They're still the only families untouched, strong and healthy."

"Did you manage to fix the starboard shuttle?"

"Only the shuttle on the port hull is fully operative. Meteors did a good job of the other."

"We needed more time. More time!"

"We might still make it," said the Captain, but then he gasped and held his throat.

The Commander turned to him. "Captain!"

The pale-faced officer run his finger around the collar of his navy tunic. "A cold sweat covers my body. My throat's closing up."

"You must get out of here immediately!"

"It came on so quickly..." he gasped. Then he struggled through the door to the ejector room.

The Commander turned to his second-in-command, the lovely Rachel, just thirty and in perfect shape and health. Has the virus reached her, he wondered.

"Rachel, I want you to arrange for the Ranyon and Kantona families to be isolated in the port shuttle. They are six in total."

There were tears trickling down her fresh, oval face. "Very good, Commander," she whispered.

"I'm sorry. The Captain had to go."

"He was always caring." She brushed her blonde hair with her hand and made for the corridor.

"Rachel, you and I are considered a threat. I don't want you touching them or getting too near."

"I understand, Commander."

"Tell them on no account must they leave the protection of the shuttle. They know the score."

As the ship continued its journey more and more lost their lives. Not just through disease but physically unable to cope with the demanding conditions and lack of food. The two isolated families were untouched by the troubles, surviving on the shuttle's supplies. Beth Ranyon was chosen to be first in command of the shuttle while Matt Kantona was deputy; both were trained to master the controls via visual transmission.

Two days later, the catamaran made its first orbit of Sunevia. For the first time the Commander felt the uncertainty of the unknown. Would there be life there? If so, would they welcome the newcomers or slay them? Fifteen people had survived the journey: the Commander, Rachel, three of the Ranyon family, three of the Kantona`s and one doctor were among them. Only the Commander, Rachel, the two families knew that the single shuttle was available.

He told the shuttle operator to stand by as the main ship entered the stratosphere. At first all went smoothly, but then the controls would not respond. The Commander and Rachel battled hard and long trying to maintain a safe entry speed, but the craft could not resist the powerful gravity of Sunevia. There came a shuddering, banging, cracking, and then an acrid smell spread through the cabin followed by a fine blue smoke.

"Initiate shuttle flight!" barked the Commander. "Release! Release!"

Rachel managed to press the release button on her console before she collapsed. Commander Eden could barely hear the energising of the shuttle's motors, but hear it he did before he too fell on the control room floor. As the shuttle sped away, the families of Ranyon and Kantona could see the catamaran breaking up then exploding in a blinding flash. The shuttle wavered, but its powerful motors stabilised and it made its way to Sunevia.

Within the troposphere, the shuttle began to heat up. As it descended mile after mile the blistering heat swept from the heat shields like a blast furnace impairing the vision of Beth Ranyon. But it remained intact diving ever closer to land and sweeping across rugged countryside. Beth scanned the terrain looking for a safe spot to land, but from wilderness to jungles, from hills to rocky tors, there was nowhere safe. A great mountain suddenly loomed forcing her to climb quickly, then ended as quickly as it came dropping sheer cliffs to the open sea. The area which the scientists had probed, photographed and considered a good place to land and live, could not be found.

"Beth, the fuel is running low," said Kantona.

"Yes yes," answered the concerned pilot. "We must not land in the middle of an ocean. We'd never survive."

Matt's fourteen-year-old son, and Beth's daughter of the same age, sat belted in their twin ejector seats. Fear lined their faces as they looked at each other through transparent helmets, their crinkling silver spacesuits rustling above the low hum of the soundproof shuttle. Nobody wanted to face the scenario of ejection and parachuting. They all believed they could land safely in the new world and enjoy the beauty of that blue sea and the green mountains. They wanted to taste fresh food, drink pure water, lie on the green lush grass and feel the warmth of the sun. Had they come all this way from clinical plastic walls, processed food and artificial living just to be buried on alien land? It seemed so, for their shuttle was losing power and the sea was never-ending. The fuel indicator dropped lower and lower, they would have to land in the water.

"I'm going to skim the surface," said Beth. "The shuttle will be transferring to emergency fuel tank shortly. If we wait until the fuel runs out, we'll drop like a lump of lead."

As she said it, the fuel ran out and the control circuits automatically tried to transfer to the emergency tank. They all looked at each other aghast as the engines cut and the constant swish of the shuttle prevailed. Beth and Matthew attempted to bring in the emergency tank manually, but nothing would respond. The shuttle was dropping at an alarming rate, twisting and banking, the sea growing ever closer.

"Brace yourselves." Beth made a short prayer and activated the multiple buttons of the ejector seats. Mercifully, the roof opened and the two fourteen year-olds shot out, screaming as they left. For some inexplicable reason the remaining ejectors did not release and the four adults were stuck in the shuttle. There were three circuits each activating two seats. Two circuits failed, leaving Beth stabbing at the controls time and time again. The drop was immediate and fast, the shuttle dived into the sea with terrific force and disappeared, hissing in an eddy of steam. The two youngsters that had been ejected felt their chairs loosening and departing from their parachutes. They descended swiftly in their chutes, staring fearfully as the ocean came closer and closer.

They landed safely in the water some distance away from where the shuttle disappeared, their buoyant suits restricting their movement, their bodies heavy and difficult to manoeuvre, a gentle undercurrent taking them away from the foamy disaster scene. The boy suddenly realised that if he didn't get to his partner they might drift and never see each other again. She had the same thought and they both used up their energy making for each other. Their gloves touched and they clasped each other like vices. Looking ahead, they could see the outline of land, and the tide was taking them there.

As they came nearer to the fine white sand the buoyancy of the water helped them to stand and wade. Then the oxygen from the boy's back-pack began to fade. He stood in the calm water chest high struggling for breath, his body heavy, his senses dulling, the transparent globe around his head misting. The girl didn't know what was happening and screamed at him as he tore at the release trigger of his headgear.

"Not yet! We must get used to the atmosphere."

The boy couldn't hear her. Besides, it was a case of die with the helmet on or trust the atmosphere of the new world to save him. They'd come this far and had to remove their protective helmets. When he threw away his helmet the atmosphere was grossly offensive to his senses: The air was pungent to his nose, the heat stung his eyes, the sun burnt his flesh, yet it was not life-threatening. He dipped his head in the sea to cool it, but the salt stung him. He tried to walk to the dryness of the shore but continually fell to his knees, crawling and gasping, splashing and reaching forward, his mind not in control, his instinct forcing him on. When he reached the sand, he lay on his stomach, his brain swirling as though it were in a jar of water.

The girl, horrified at seeing it all, remained chest high in the water calling to him. She went silent as she saw her last companion struggling and gasping on the sand. If he is to die, then she might as well join him, their skeletons witness to the inhabitants of Sunevia that people from the stars came and died. As she made her way to the shore, she realised her friend's breathing was slowing and becoming less violent. Then he pushed hard on his hands, raised his body and turned to her.

"I think it's going to be all right," he gasped. "The pressure in my head is subsiding, though my body feels very heavy." He attempted to stand but fell back. He tried it a few times until he struggled to his feet, his knees bending, his arms leaden at his sides. He called to her.

"The gravity is going to take some getting used to. Come on out of the water but take it slowly."

Once out, she kept her spacesuit on as they slowly and arduously made their way inland. The place was surely a paradise, thick with luxuriant growth of fruit trees and herbaceous shrubs. Wild flowers of many colours kept them ogle-eyed. At times, they would recoil when a small animal jumped from tree to tree, or another darted from a hole in the ground. Occasionally the girl opened and closed neutralising valves, getting her senses used to the atmospheric conditions. The boy walked a little easier in his green thin tunic and trousers after discarding his spacesuit. Eventually, the girl gained confidence and removed her suit, and she walked easier in her turquoise slip and top.

"What perfumes, what beautiful scents. Even the air tastes sweet."

Coming to a clearing, where a brook sparkled as it jinked down a wooded bank, they stopped in wonder at seeing the beauty of flowing water. Not having consumed liquid for many hours, they were tempted to take a drink. The boy held his hand up.

"We'll have to be careful of what we eat and drink, even though I feel I could throw myself into that hollow the stream runs through."

"Look," she said, amazed at an elegant animal emerging from the woods. It bent its delicate neck and drank from the pool. "It must be all right to drink."

They watched the animal take its fill. It looked up and saw them, turned and disappeared back into the shade of the foliage.

The girl bent down and cupped her hands filling them with water. She drank a little at first, then nodded to the boy and drank some more.

"It runs over my tongue cold but sweet. It's wonderful."

He joined her and they drank together. Then the girl walked to a tree bearing fruit and plucked one.

"Careful," he warned. But she tasted and the juice ran from her lips.

"It's good. Some great Power has guided us to food, water and warmth. What the Power has given will not harm us."

"I hope you're right. I wonder if there are inhabitants here."

"If there are I hope they're wiser than our civilisation."

They looked at each other realising the responsibility they had been given.

The boy said, "Was it an accident that we were the only survivors?"

"Maybe we have been chosen."

He gazed into her blue eyes. "Maybe. If we are the only ones here, we'll have to start all over again."

Other books by Ken James

Gerwyn's Problems ISBN: 978-0-9928690-4-5

Anna from Hay ISBN: 978-0-9568031-7-7

When The Kids Grow Up